Adventures

of a

Space Bum

Book 4

The Palace Guard

by

Jon Batson

Midnight Whistler Publishers – since 1979

First Edition

ISBN-13:9780989372640
ISBN-10:0989372642

Midnight Whistler Publishers
midnightwhistler@gmail.com

Cover Art by

What they're saying about
THE PALACE GUARD

Prolific author Jon Batson returns to his popular series
"Adventures of a Space Bum." Improved over time like a fine
wine, the wonderful narrative voice Jon uses throughout the
series highlights his entertaining storytelling style.

You can tell Jon loves his setting, characters, and story, from
how well he writes them. He weaves the detailed worlds
together and brings the interesting characters to life in my
head. It is such fun to read!

Our heroine's efforts to stay off the collective radar of the
authorities and underworld, has of course drawn their
increasing attention.

"We keep hoping for a quiet, predictable journey, without
hair-raising stories to tell, but we have yet to experience that."
Now our plucky Captain Starwort has attracted the greedy
interest of outright pirates, and the oppressive Central
Government. Both have thrown the full power and bullying
might of their lead ships at collecting her, dead or alive—her
exotic ship and fabled fortune as well.

I do not know how this petite young woman, "demure as all
hell," keeps getting out of worlds of trouble. I think, between
the stars, she plays music for the Fates.

Michael Nelson, Author

Some series lose their momentum over time, but not "Adventures of A Space Bum." This series keeps getting better and better with each book. Besides having the most lovable space pirates since the TV series Firefly, Starwort's adventures are filled with laughter, drama, mayhem, and even a bit of romance! I must admit, I felt a touch of melancholy when book 4 came to an end, because I was not ready to stop reading. I'll be eagerly awaiting book 5!

Robin Walls, **Blogger and Life Coach**

Tyrannical governments, the eternal quest for freedom from such, treachery, holograms and sentient space ships, heroes and villains, believable characters; all here. Jon Batson is a wordsmith who weaves an interplanetary adventure injecting just the right amount of humor and insightful quips into the human condition. A most enjoyable read. I didn't want it to end.

Diann Haist, Artist and Avid Reader

A very enjoyable read. Jon Batson gets better with every book he writes. And he set the bar pretty high to begin with. Starwort continues her journey, which has taken her so far from a helpless waif to a budding superhero. Batson weaves character, action and plot seamlessly. Put down your X-box and pick up this book.

Steven Gary Schlussel - world-class entertainer

I loved the fast pace movement in The Palace Guard, I felt as though I was on board flax with all the others. It amazes me when I read today's news of what is going on with our world how this Sci-Fi becomes more like reality. The Palace Guard is a fantastic read!

Nancy Long - Business Owner

Adventures of a Space Bum

book 4

The Palace Guard

Glossary

Abigail	Starwort's friend from school, deceased
Aristaeus	Doctor Genus, named for the Greek god, son of Apollo
Augur	A seer, fortune teller
Baal	Hindu deity. When used with "son of" or "in the name of" it is profanity
Bacchus	Starwort's family name, in Greek and Roman mythology, god of wine. Also, home planet named for the family Bacchus
Behemoth	A huge or monstrous creature
Borth	A large and angry dog used to guard locations. (Borth stool: what this animal leaves behind him)
Cecrops	A planet with two cities: Daedalus and Icarus
Chineel	First mate, Starwort's aunt, named for the Manchineel flower
CG	Central Government of Earth, an oppressive body
Cyrene 21X	A long range space vehicle
Chandler	Purveyor of ship's goods and supplies
Copernicus	A town named for Copernicus, the founder of modern astronomy
Dagon	Philistine fish-god, name of Starwort's crewman.

Daphne   School friend of Starwort's, still living on
             Khons, the home planet

Daughter of Sixes! Profanity – child of the devil

Daughters, the   nickname for the islands of Sterope

Demon Urchin   Profanity – child of the devil

Fangdu   Short for Fangdu Kouzhao & Fangdu
             Shoutao, matching surgical mask and glove
             sets

Flax   Name of Starwort's vessel, after a flower
             meaning benefactor "I will call you Flax, for
             you are my benefactor"

Galium   Friend from Sterope, named for a flower
             signifying rudeness

Grecian Flu   Illness created by the Central Government
             to control the population

Hermes   In Greek mythology, messenger of the gods,
             in this story, a GPS unit, a tracking device

Hovermags   Magnets set into the bottom of a vehicle to
             make it hover and move

Indran Storm   Hurricane-force storm

Be-demoned!   Exclamation of having erred in judgment

Khons   A planet named for the Egyptian god of the
             chase; Starwort's home planet

Mithra Tavern   A tavern on Sterope, named after a
             goddess worshiped as the mediator

Morning Ale   A non-alcoholic morning energy drink

New Babylon   A planet with both low-life bars and
             healing pools

RRD   Remote Repair Drone

Seb   President of the Central Government on
             Earth

Semper Adonis   A name used by Galium, from Semper, Latin for Forever, and Adonis, the name of a beautiful Roman god

Shu   A planet named for the Greek god of the air

Starwort   Name of a low-growing north temperate herb having small white star-shaped flowers; has an alleged ability to ease sharp pains in the side. Meaning: afterthought

Sterope   An island on New Babylon, named after one of the Pleiades

Trebium Scuttle   A part no longer used on space vessels

Universals   Denomination of money common to all worlds, using the symbol Ц, as in Ц20

Victoriana   The planet where Dr. Genus lives

Wind Pools   Expensive resort at New Babylon, famous for its healing vapors

Starwort (stärwôrt) n. Any of various water plants having star-shaped flowers. Also, low-growing north temperate herb; named for its ability to ease sharp pains in the side. Significance: Afterthought

"I got a tattoo: a tiny, white, star-shaped flower on my left shoulder blade. It was to remind me that I am a weed growing in still waters. So I kept moving, avoiding the still waters; vowing to be a weed no more."
Starwort Bacchus

Icarus in Flames

"Senior Sergeant Phaetone!" bellowed the commanding officer of the Icarus Constabulary, Captain Vikare. He stood at his office door, glaring into the common room of the Icarus headquarters. His right hand tapped against his left behind his back. On his chest he wore a ribbon of periwinkle blue, adorned with a tiny, pearled platinum, Icarus seven-pointed star. The medal had been awarded him for his recent apprehension of Datur Minot and his circle of criminals. A desk-full of unsolved crimes had been closed in a day with the explosion of the spire in the city of Daedalus.

"He's in the Communication Tower, Sir," said Sergeant Ariadne, looking up from her reader. The young sergeant also wore the blue ribbon with the Icarus star. She had behaved bravely during the recent events in Daedalus and served him well now.

Vikare sighed, pulling his lips into his mouth. He wished he could make Ariadne his senior sergeant instead of that trebium-scuttle, Phaeton.

"Call him, sergeant, and be sure to use his full title: Senior Sergeant. You know how he gets."

Sergeant Ariadne let a tiny smile slip through her professional exterior as she turned away to attend to the calling of the Senior Sergeant.

Ariadne had been the smallest in her class, Captain Vikare reflected, and as a result had something to prove. She was also the smartest in her class. She was the first to arrive, the last to leave and the one to call if you wanted anything done right. She could shoot straight and true if needed, but was also the best choice to break bad news to family members. She was the one he would have chosen, if Phaeton hadn't made sergeant before her. It was a flawed system.

The blood left Vikare's face as Senior Sergeant Phaeton came striding into the common room, the full Icarus Star medal pinned to his chest. The seven-pointed, pearl-platinum star was as large as a man's palm. Each medal received by the Constabulary consisted of a full medal and a matching ribbon to be worn on the daily uniform.

No tiny ribbons for S. S. Phaeton! No, sir! The medal entered the room before he did. The reflection of light from the Icarus Star lit up the common room as if in preparation for his coming.

Senior Sergeant Phaeton was energized! Captain Vikare was mortified!

"Sir!" snapped S. S. Phaeton.

"Assemble the staff, Sergeant."

"Senior Sergeant," corrected Phaeton.

"What?"

"It's Senior Sergeant, sir." Phaeton lifted a finger to indicate the bar beneath the chevron on his left sleeve. The additional bar, sewn with silver thread, indicated that the rank above had been raised to a senior level, but not enough to indicate a promotion to a higher rank.

"Yes, of course. Please assemble the staff," Vikare took a breath. "Senior Sergeant Phaeton."

The captain rolled his eyes as Phaeton turned in place, affected a similar stance to his captain and raised his voice to be heard above the rumble of actual work getting done.

"Attention! Attention! The Captain has an announcement."

Phaeton turned to his Captain. He smiled with a nod, indicating that the staff was ready; he could now proceed with his announcement.

"Thank you, Senior Sergeant."

Phaeton stepped back, confident that he had properly prepared the room for something important. Captain

Vikare took a step forward. He sucked in a large quantity of air and delivered the edict in a low, resigned voice.

"The Central Government is coming to Cecrops. Headquarters will be established in Daedalus with a local HQ in Icarus. Recent events have drawn their attention and it has been decided that not enough control has been exerted over our little planet."

The room froze as some constables glanced at others with wide eyes. A few let out a horrified gasp, a couple sucked in a mouthful of air and one new constable in the back fainted.

"An urgent transmission has been received concerning a vessel that recently left Cecrops for Victoriana. Flagged as a pirate vessel, Exterra Bacchus is to be apprehended and taken into custody, it's captain and crew placed under bond. I will be looking for volunteers to ..."

The Captain paused as every hand in the room, save for S.S. Phaeton and the unconscious constable, went up to volunteer. Vikare continued.

"... volunteers to undertake this difficult and dangerous mission. I only need three. Sergeant Ariadne, would you please choose three volunteers for the mission to apprehend these criminals?"

Captain Vikare turned back to his office as Ariadne chose three of the eager volunteers pressing her to become her best friend.

"Captain?" said Phaeton, following him into his office. "Uh, sir, surely I'll be one of those going with you."

"No, Phaeton, you'll be here, receiving the officials of the Central Government and running this office. I expect with the CG here, there won't be a lot to do, so you'll be fine. Congratulations, Senior Sergeant. At last, you're in charge."

The Captain closed his door, with S.S. Phaeton standing outside, the frosted glass nearly touching his nose.

"Do you expect anything to still be here when you return?" said a voice from the corner.

"It will be here, Sector Agent, but it won't be the same. It will never be the same again."

Honor Toth stepped from the corner. "That's treason, you know."

"The answer or the question?"

"Both," said Honor. He smiled. He knew, as the captain knew, that anything even slightly derisive regarding the Central Government was forbidden. The reaction of the men in the common room, the constable who fainted, even Phaeton requesting to go rather than stay; all were treasonous.

"Will you stay and continue the search for the fugitive, Galium?"

"Yes, Captain. I've no choice. My office has supported

the CG's suggestion that I lead the hunt. Orders reinforcing the assignment arrived soon after the initial order."

"I'm sure criminals all over the rim are heaving a sigh of relief at the news."

"Yes, there is rejoicing in many quadrants. While I am here, I cannot be there. It would be considered a vacation, were it not for the Central Government watchdogs over my shoulder at every turn. They'll make sure I stay busy."

"You've worked with the CG before, then."

"In proximity; no one works 'with' the CG. One always works 'for' the CG, and it's never good enough, quick enough or clever enough."

"Yes, I've noted. I'm glad I won't be here."

"Why are you going? Surely not to actually apprehend Captain Bacchus and her crew."

"And why not? There is an alert on the airwaves, the orders are explicit. Exterra Bacchus even altered flight plans after departure. That raises suspicion, don't you think?"

"I'm under orders, Captain. I don't think."

The Sector Agent and the Captain exchanged knowing glances. The conversation was over. It would be forgotten. In fact, it never happened. The Sector Agent slipped out of the side door, into the growing winds of the coming storm.

"There is indeed a storm coming," reflected the Captain. "The recent Indran storm will pale in comparison."

Knock, knock! The door to the captain's office opened. Sergeant Ariadne walked to the desk and snapped to attention.

"Sir, the volunteers have been chosen."

"Any problems?"

"No sir, they are the ones you requested."

"And do you agree?"

"Yes, sir. They are the same ones I would have chosen."

"You did choose them, Sergeant."

Ariadne smiled. Vikare looked at her with one brow raised, his mouth lifting slightly in the corner. They spoke a secret language these days, conspirators concealed by uniforms and medals.

"You'd better pack, Ariadne. We'll be lifting off as soon as transport is fueled and stocked."

"How long do you foresee this mission taking, Captain?"

"As long as it takes, Ariadne, as long as it takes."

Exterra Bacchus

"It will be good to see Khons again," I said to Flax. I was sitting on the bridge watching the stars and contemplating life, enjoying being in soft clothes for a change, my summer skirt and light blouse. I held the clarinet, though I hadn't played it yet.

"Yes, it will, though we will not be going there first," replied Flax.

"Not Khons?"

"That is correct, Star. We will not be going to Khons immediately. First, there will be a stop at Victoriana. Doctor Genus wants to run a diagnostic on my systems after recent events."

Flax's holographic head turned to look out at the

blackness before us, speckled with a million stars, each different from the others and each with a story to tell.

Khons had been our destination, where we would find the answer to the latest set of riddles posed by the elusive Galium. Victoriana was some distance away, even with the Red Stroke Drive at cruising speed. I had time to reflect upon the stars and planets before us.

Many of the stars, I knew, were not there at all, but suns that burned out eons earlier, their light just now reaching us. Time was a relative thing. Flax was a repair vessel, at one time automated to remove the necessity for a crew, then refitted by Doctor Genus to allow for her new crew. This was, in fact, her third life. I was younger still, just a few seasons out of school, and yet we were all flying along together, the stars, the ship and the girl. It was poetic, though if you pressed me to explain it, I could not.

"A change in destination?" asked Chineel, slipping into the co-pilot's seat, still in her apron from the galley. Her hair, a mass of red tangles, was pulled back out of her face, though many strands escaped to reach for her eyes and mouth.

"Victoriana. Take out your crinolines."

"I don't mind. I'm ready for some time being pretty and quiet. I could also stand being well fed. The doctor always sets a grand table."

"That he does. I have to say, after the chases we have endured, I am ready to relax in Victoriana's turn-of-the-century ambiance."

Chineel breathed a sigh of agreement. The stars flickered, some of the nearer ones moving as we flew by at Red Stroke speed. I snickered. Chineel turned. I felt the need to explain.

"They don't move, we do. The stars aren't flying by us, we are flying by them. I was just thinking, that's all."

"Taking the time to think. That's something we haven't done in a while."

"Mmm," I replied.

Flax raised her head, as if attentive after being relaxed. My muscles tightened. I knew it was too good to be true. Something was amiss. Was it Icarus behind us, Victoriana before us, Galium who had just left us or the Sector Agent who stayed to guard our departure?

"What is it, Flax?"

"An alert has gone out for a rogue Exterra class vessel carrying pirates. The Central Government has taken an increased interest in Cecrops, in the recent happenings in Daedalus and Icarus."

"Honor is still there," I said, with a noticeable quake in my voice.

"He is searching for the fugitive Galium. He makes daily forays into the city with local constables. He is putting on a grand show. I have no doubt he will continue to make a fine display for the Central Government."

"That may not be so easy. They're not outer-rim constables. The CG chooses their agents by a different set of criteria. They always look for the most suspicious and untrusting people to put on the front lines."

"Galium has alluded them at every turn. He will continue to do so on Cecrops, even with Honor Toth on his trail."

Chineel could not keep quiet longer. "Wait! Isn't Galium on his way to Copernicus disguised as the attorney, Semper Adonis?"

Flax and I both turned to regard Chineel. She had apparently missed the fine subtleties of Galium's disguise.

"OK, Chineel. In order to appear in public and with constables there, Galium assumed an identity, that of an attorney with the ridiculous name of Semper Adonis. He said he was from Copernicus and would be returning there, but he clearly won't. They'll do a check and find no Semper Adonis listed in the registry, then they'll see if there's anyone going to Copernicus and so on until they've expended tremendous resources in a search that turns up nothing. Galium is off in the universe to parts unknown. He'll contact us when the time is right."

"Oh," said Chineel. "Well, all right then."

My thoughts turned to Galium, rude, wonderful Galium, who called me "Little Wort" though I asked him not to, but who always looked out for me, no matter what. I pictured him flying in his shiny new Cyrene 21X to ports unknown, places where he could slip in under the spectral search beam and blend in with the locals.

These were the thoughts that filled my head as I sat on the bridge watching our progress and again later as I slipped off to sleep.

Meeting Galium

Still a young girl just escaped from school, I stood in the open door of the Mithra Tavern in the low islands of Sterope on the planet of New Babylon, hungry, dirty and cold. My hair was matted, my clothes were soiled and hung loose on my frame. One wet and grimy stocking sagged limp around my left ankle.

"What have the Daughters brought us?" a cheery, chuckling voice said. It belonged to a smiling man with a white beard fringing his round face. "Is there a gypsy caravan passing through Sterope? We should tell them they have lost an imp, one too young to travel alone."

It was true: I was just a girl, improperly out of school.

13.

The first signs of womanhood had yet to appear on me, I was still in the braids of childhood.

"A waif, Papa Posei," said a blond woman, dressed the trousers of a man with a loose-fitting blouse of white silk. "By the look of her, she could use a meal and a bath."

"Than she shall have both," said the man with a full, black beard leaning out from behind the blond woman. "But which first? Jessamine, you decide."

"A little of both, Galium, just to be on the safe side. Come little waif, you need to scrub those hands before you touch food."

The blond woman called Jessamine ushered me with a slender hand to a refresh room. I was not in the mood to protest, not with food, any food, as the prize.

"Where do you come from, young princess?"

She brought me to the wash bowl and indicated the soap, guessing I was not so young that I didn't know what to do next. As I picked up the soap, she poured the water into the bowl from the pitcher, letting it flow over my hands. It was cold.

"Khons," I squeaked, too soft for the authorities to hear.

"A long way to travel. What is your name, princess?"

"Starwort," I said and plunged my face into the icy water. At last, I thought, perhaps I will not die of thirst and hunger, perhaps I will only be killed by pirates here in Sterope.

It had been a long journey. The blue jacket and gray skirt of my school uniform showed the miles. They were clean and pressed when I bid the Vesta Academy for Young Ladies a hasty farewell.

It was the end of the year. Graduation loomed and I was to be one of the leading students, surpassing expectation. Still, graduation was not possible.

The headmaster summed up my situation: "The problem is two-fold. On the one hand, you have no family. Your parents and your uncle, as you know, are deceased."

The second half of the equation was the clincher; I was also out of money.

"There is nothing left in your trust fund. Your father's gift has run out. Without money, I'm afraid you cannot remain at Vesta Academy and certainly cannot represent the school as valedictorian. You understand."

I did understand. For the crime of having no money left, and no family as well, I was to be sent to the central state school. A representative had come to collect me, a man with a look I had only seen on pictures of hunting cats.

"And who is this?" he said, preparing to take custody. His hand twitched at his side and his eyes widened. He was all but licking his lips with delight.

"Miss Starwort Bacchus. She is a standout and promises to finish well, but there is no family to present her and no money left in her fund to complete the year. It is a problem."

"Bacchus? Doctor Bacchus? Your parents held land. There is a vast holding to which you have a map and many deeds. There is said to be accounts brimming with money as yet untouched."

Based upon that supposition alone, both men made a decision: My father's fortune, whatever was left, whatever could be found, would be monitored on my behalf. Monitored! I heard it as "stolen" and my behalf did not come into play at all. Both men shook hands. Both men counted upon my father's fortune being more than even my uncle could spend before his untimely end.

The same night, I packed my worldly possessions into a single bag, took one final look behind me and slipped through the back fence to the road.

I was not yet out of earshot when I heard the alarm sound. Apparently, one or both of them had come into my room after bedtime to make certain I was safe and properly tucked in.

For a while I stayed with a friend, hiding at her house from imagined agents of the school. Daphne and I sat on our beds until the wee hours talking like we once did in school, sharing our hopes and dreams. In the mornings, we sat in the back yard, not too far from the watchful eyes of her parents, and ventured farther than we should have in the afternoons when they tired of watching us.

Secretly, one overcast afternoon, Daphne and I went into the far part of town where no one of quality would go, a place not for young ladies, to the Body Art tattoo parlor. A tiny flower bloomed on Daphne's shoulder blade, the Daphne Mezereum to remind her she might be a little too eager to please. On my own shoulder blade, I had the man draw the white flower growing in still waters, the flower with the power to heal a pain in the side, the Starwort. It would remind me to not stay too long in still waters, lest they turn stagnant.

When Daphne's house turned stagnant, I left and traveled to the low islands of New Babylon where I heard no one asked or cared about your past.

My skin was so dry the water stung, yet felt soothing, as if I could be reborn in the wash bowl. Within its cooling waters I would rise refreshed and renewed, clean and glowing. I would become a daughter of the Siren Islands: Sterope, Terpsichore, Melpomene and the new one, me, the isle of Starwort. I would become a Winged Maiden and there live with Papa Posie, Jessamine and Galium.

Jessamine pulled me up from the water bowl by my dirty collar, sputtering and gasping for air. In my enthusiasm I had forgotten to breathe.

"All things in bits and pieces, child. Food first, then a full bath. This is no time for drowning; remember to breathe." It was good advice.

Jessamine watched me intently as I toweled my face and hands, ensuring the dust of the planets I had traveled no longer lingered.

"Starwort! It's a flower, isn't it?"

I nodded. I didn't know her well enough to show her the tattoo on my shoulder blade, unseemly for a girl my age. I did know her name, however. Jessamine was named for the Jasmine flower, which could be the common white variety, which signified amiability. She was amiable. But if it was for the Spanish variety, it signified sensuality. She could easily have that facet as well. One can be both sensual and amiable. In fact, considered, both at once would be desirable.

Naming children after the flowers of Earth, with their meanings and hope for what traits the child might take on, or in ignorance of them in some cases, was common, especially in the middle ring planets.

"Afterthought." My voice trailed off.

"What, what's that, Starwort?"

"Afterthought," I said, stronger. "My name means afterthought, as yours means amiability, or sensuality. I'm not sure which. It could be both."

Jessamine nodded, her eyes wide and empty. She didn't seem to understand what I was talking about. I guessed she didn't know her name was for a flower and the flower had significance, as all did.

"Let's get some food into you, so you'll begin making sense. Galium and Papa Posei will have a plate ready."

Jessamine looked at my skirt, hanging loose around my waist. It would have remained still had I spun too quickly in a circle, I had grown so thin. My stocking dangling limp at my ankle and my blouse hung limp from my shoulders.

Jassemine shook her head and opened the wardrobe where her own clothing hung. She took my dirty clothes and gave me her dressing gown to wear. She rolled the sleeves and stepped back to look at me.

"Demure as all hell!" she said. Her smile told me it was her way of being light-hearted. I smiled for the first time since I had arrived.

Galium, the man named for the flower signifying rudeness, did have a plate for me. He pointed at a chair.

"Her name is Starwort. She's named for a flower," said Jessamine, as if she had uncovered a bit of precious information.

"Then come along, Little Wort, and have some of Iberis's fine stew. It'll put meat back on those bones." Galium looked me up and down, a waif in a borrowed dressing gown.

"Starwort," I said, with a glance at Galium.

"Eh, Little Wort? What's that?"

"Starwort! Not Wort or Little Wort. I am named after a flower of Earth, the Starwort." My glance took on a sharp facet. I was a girl, but not to be poked if one was fond of one's fingers.

"Oh! And does the Starwort flower have thorns?" said Galium.

"Be mindful, gentlemen! This one has a barb," added Papa Posei, named for Poseidon, the god of the sea.

There was laughter all around the Mithra Tavern. In the middle of the assembled group of philosophers, poets and pirates sat the littlest pirate of them all, spooning stew made by Galium's friend, Iberis, named after the flower signifying indifference, who didn't care if I liked her stew or not.

After I left Mithra Tavern, I traveled, sometimes with others, sometimes alone, often at the last minute and with my worldly belongings in a pillow cover. Taking to the road with empty pockets was preferable to staying in comfort when my life was in danger.

After a few months of difficult times on Copernicus, I left just as suddenly and just as out of options. The landlord wanted his rent and I had none. Desperate times call for desperate measures. As my desperate act, I climbed out of the window, across the town roofs and roads until I found the sky dock. I chose the only available vehicle as my escape pod from Copernicus.

The door was about to close, I had no time for discussion. I clambered aboard as it took off, moments before constables could lay hands on me.

My benefactor was an automated repair vehicle, run by a computer with no name, but only a ship's designation: Exterra 4136A, Automated Repair Vessel, Outer Reaches, Fourth Quadrant. I named the vessel Flax, for the flower signifying benefactor. We have become friends.

In time, Exterra 4136A became Exterra Bacchus, no longer bound to receive repair contracts from a distant office run by an absentee owner. She became her own vessel with me as her Captain.

The Kraken

Pytho, Captain of the Kraken, had chosen the name of the vessel carefully. Kraken, in Earth history was the many-armed creature that could bring down all ships.

Standing on the bridge of the Free Vessel Kraken, Pytho smiled. He saw himself as a giant monster, overcoming and devouring all who stumbled into his path. The mighty Central Government could not find or apprehend Pytho. He had evaded them at every turn. He was invincible and would rule space as did the Kraken of old.

"Khons in our wake, Captain. Next stop: Juno on the planet Jove."

"No, Agni, Jove was never our destination. Set sail for

Victoriana."

"Mighty high security measures on Victoriana, Captain."

"I'm aware, Agni. We're going there anyway. The prize, in this instance, is worth the risk."

Captain Pytho chuckled privately. Agni was named for the ancient Earth god of India, the god of fire. However, Agni's fire had gone out, there was no glow from his eyes.

Pytho looked down at his ill-named first mate. He stood head and shoulders above the cringing pirate before him. He'd saved Agni from execution while stealing a large treasure held in the same underground dungeon. Saving the treasure meant taking the man as well. There were days when he wondered if he made the right choice.

"Setting course for Victoriana, Captain," said Agni, slinking away to the wheelhouse, where he was protected from the Captain's evil eye.

Pytho leaned into the long-range viewer. He pressed his shoulders against the pads, straining his eye to see farther than the complex lenses allowed, all the way to Victoriana. He looked away just long enough to ensure that the packet he had paid so dearly for was still on his desk. Three crewmen were lost and four more wounded to obtain the packet, bound in old leather, now outlawed - not that he cared - and tied with a ragged piece of thong. The leathery thong was said to be cut from the skin of a criminal who had died trying to get his hands on the treasure within. The criminal's name was Osiris. He was, according to legend, dropped from an airship into the local marketplace, impaled on the central flagpole, his arms outstretched as if asking forgiveness, forgiveness that would never come.

Pytho liked the stories behind the legends, the histories of the items that had come within his grasp, each with a tale to tell and each more horrific than the last. That the leather packet was tied with a strip of the skin of a pirate who had himself become impaled on a spike after being dropped from a vessel into the market was too colorful and juicy for him to resist. He had to find the captain of that vessel, the adversary who bested such a villainous thief. He tried to picture Osiris, who was said to be eight feet tall and black as coal, with arms of steel and legs of cast iron. He was sure the stories were enhanced with each telling, but surely there must be some truth.

Who, he wondered, pushed the mighty Osiris, named for the god of the Sun in ancient Earth mythology, out of a bay door? Whose fortune was this and how was Osiris connected? Most importantly, how was he bested? What great beast or monstrous pirate could have bested the mighty Osiris?

Pytho tapped the console to his left and looked at the

display. Plenty of time. The enhanced plasma drive was at cruising speed and would get them to Victoriana in good time. All was as it should be.

He sat at the desk and opened the packet. The smell of old leather wafted up into his nostrils, causing him to smile.

The packet had been put together by one who had thoroughly researched the treasure described in the journal. He was said to have later been slain by a child, stung in the eye with a blade.

The child was said to be magic, accompanied by a witch and a sorceress, both magical. He didn't believe a word, of course, but he loved the telling of the tales.

One pirate king was sent screaming from a window onto a street filled with constables.

Another was struck in the face with a hot frying pan, blinding him and marking him for life – a life that was short-lived.

Still another was said to have fired upon the original owner of the treasure and struck his own woman instead, killing her.

The giant Osiris snapped the neck of another, rather like that of a chicken. The snapping of the neck occurred minutes before Osiris himself fell from the vessel that lifted him to the sky in escape. The escape proved to be a phantom, disappearing in the mist as a dream. They were as spoken words on a winter's day, a puff of smoke, here within grasp, then gone leaving no trace.

Pytho rolled the old legends around in his head, loving the colorful exaggerations and heightened expectations. He longed to meet the survivors of such tales, the heroes of the legends. And at the same time, he thought, no, he would not. They would be small and stupid, having stumbled into a unique set of circumstances. By now they would be old and wizened, their best days behind them, their treasure spent. No, he would not meet the heroes of these stories, any more than he would meet the villains. He opened the packet. At least these were what they were and could not be embellished.

What he found were copies, not originals. Some were bad copies, faded and aged, some torn, wrinkled and ripped as in a fight. Each item in the packet told a tale. A large folio unrolled to show a dead face, the power sources burned out long before, replacements having gone out of production in favor of newer, improved though incompatible, power source. His engineer would have to rig something if this folio was to give up its secrets.

A stack of single document slats fell out, similar to readers, but older, reminiscent of the school slats of his youth.

Pytho had spent enough time in school to learn that it

was useless to him. There was no need to work for what he wanted, he could steal it easier. But the slats of his youth held lessons for school boys. These slender slats held deeds and the locations of treasure.

One was a deed to a great house on Khons. The address had been corrupted and was unreadable, but it was on Khons and in the central metropolis, not the rural lands surrounding. Another was a planet, said to be beyond the outer rim on the other side of the galaxy. Nothing seemed to be near this planet, so it could be of little value or great value, depending upon its future use. As a colony, being far from everyone has its advantages, especially if staying off the grid from the Central Government is your plan. On the other hand, supply routes are few the far between on the outer rim and supplies are therefore expensive.

There were other slats, other deeds, several bank documents, all digital, all slat-mounted. Some had weak power sources and flickered or faded. Others were dead completely.

One still bright and glowing showed a vessel. The vessel was said to be the most valuable item in the packet. Pytho pondered this one as stranger than all the rest. There was one picture of a giant ship, bursting with guns and menacing. Another showed a small and aging vessel reminiscent of a discarded seed pod, having been picked up by the wind and dumped on the ground. One of them might be an accurate representation of the vessel in question. Either would be slow in the dark, as both were built before Red Stroke Drive was created. Retrofits were expensive and difficult. Few harbors could upgrade an older vessel, especially the Exterra class, without extending the cost of the retrofit beyond the price of a new vessel.

It was a puzzle. Pytho pondered the wisdom of even looking for the vessels, as they were probably the source of legend rather than real ships.

And then there was the money. Ah, yes! The money was amazing!

Accounts on Copernicus, on Khons, on Serapis - all brimming with Universals. Tales of a box filled with Universal Trading Bonds, good forever at any exchange port, as well as gems. Gems were easily transported and of higher value than their weight in Universals. Even with the recent discoveries on Shu and the planets of the far ring, with fields of diamonds, emeralds and other exotic stones, the value of gems was great and their mobility prized. A large box of them would be - Pytho felt a chill. Just the thought of it filled him with a delight bordering on sexual. In fact, he did, just at the thought of it, become...

"Captain?" said Agni from the door. "Do you want an

update on the condition of the injured crew members?"

"No! Just see that they are ready when we reach Victoriana. And leave me alone."

Agni closed the door and retreated down the hallway. Pytho settled back with his packet, slowed his breathing and ran his hands over the folio, the slats and the torn, aging documents before him. He lowered his eyelids and whispered to the contents of the packet: "Now! Where were we?"

Victoriana

"Inside, all of you. Don't look out until you see Serapis on your screen."

Doctor Aristaeus Genus, one of Victoriana's leading citizens and a genius in his own right, was breaking the law. He was helping his household staff and several complete households of his neighbors escape from Victoriana to Serapis, a smaller place, further out on the rim of planets and not yet gobbled up by the Central Government.

Aristaeus stepped back from the over-packed interplanetary vessel and got into the bright yellow roadster convertible driven by his man, Runyon. The car took off at an unexpected speed and without the usual clattering and coughing associated with it.

Runyon usually drove the roadster at a proper and historic fifteen miles per hour, complete with a soundtrack of pistons and gears emanating from under the hood.

The effect was complete, but not for today. Today it was not necessary. No one was on the street to notice the Doctor passing. If they had been, they would have understood that the pretext, while grand and glorious, was over. Victoriana was no longer the showcase for slower living, a gentler time, when men tipped their hats to ladies with parasols. The band no longer played in the gazebo in the middle of town and the helmeted constables were no longer the peacekeepers. The Central Government had come and was in the painful process of taking over.

Runyon took the final turn on two tires. "Sorry, Sir," he said to Dr. Genus.

"That's all right, Runyon. This is her last trip anyway."

Aristaeus pressed a button and the large garage door fell away, two sides split and folded back allowing Runyon to pull the roadster into its slot.

In the next space sat a silver sphere perched on four struts from the lower side. It had been stolen from the first CG agents to land. They appeared friendly and wanting to fit in, hoping for a smooth transition wherever possible. They were respectful and asked politely. Any request not immediately fulfilled, however, was met with the disappearance of the person asked. As a result, the next request was filled immediately. The second wave of agents was not so accommodating.

As Runyon closed the great doors, he paused briefly to give the old roadster a final look, one small bit of sadness and then he would not think of it again.

Runyon took the bags sitting just inside the door connecting to the house and loaded them into the rear, higher door of the silver sphere. The last to go in, the first to come out at the other end of the sphere's final journey, were the four silver cases with combination locks.

"Final sweep, Runyon."

"Yes, sir." Runyon began with the front entry way, making sure that nothing had been left behind in any room. They would not return to this house.

Aristaeus was in his work room, his laboratory, the birthplace of his inventions. His inventions, his creations, were his children and he loved them. In the center of the workroom stood a tall, stately woman with fair, brown hair and soft, hazel eyes. She wore a long dress with a high waist and buttoned up to the throat, accompanied by gloves of soft calfskin fixed with a button at the wrist. She held a parasol and wore a large ladies hat with a gigantic feather, tied with a scarf at the chin. She turned to the Doctor and smiled.

"Are we ready, Aristaeus?"

"Yes, I believe we are. This is a day for liberation for us all, even you. Are you ready?"

"Yes, Doctor, I'm ready."

"All right, then. In you go."

Aristaeus opened a silver box, pushed the button on the left of the control panel and looked up at the lady, who smiled demurely and faded away.

Convergence

"Victoriana, Captain. Aristaeus is coming to meet us at the far end of the sky port."

"Yellow roadster, Flax?" I asked.

The four-door convertible that bounced us up and down on the road into town, coughing smoke and sounding like the pieces were unsecured under the hood, was one of my fondest memories of Victoriana. I had grown to like the ride.

I had often considered wrapping up the pieces of our puzzle and retiring to Victoriana to live out my years in the company of Aristaeus and his turn-of-the-century town. I would wear hoop skirts and mesh gloves. The great hat would shade my eyes from the sun and the yellow roadster would transport us to and from the concerts in the park on Sunday afternoon. I could live like that.

"No, he said to look for the land-sphere, it's a limited troop-carrier."

"I remember, they are a new development, but having one and not being a Central Government agent is against the law, it's not like him."

"I believe desperate times call for desperate measures," said Flax.

"I've heard that," I replied, smiling. It was, in fact, the story of my life.

"Setting down, Captain. There's the sphere."

On the far horizon, a single silver sphere came toward us. We settled onto the sky port, ready to meet with my old friend, Aristaeus.

The sphere came hurtling at us like a shot bullet. I was afraid it might not stop but go straight through us. At the final hundred yards, the silver bullet slowed and stopped at the aft port. It settled on struts and four doors lifted at once. Aristaeus stepped out and spoke to us, one arm raised in greeting.

"Hello, hello, one and all, no niceties this morning, time is of the essence. Open up, Flax, I have a surprise for you."

The aft bay opened, revealing a complex system of gadgetry reflecting the best of the doctor's genius. I looked over his shoulder as he placed a new box into a predetermined spot and attached several leads.

"Or rather, I have you as a surprise," he added. I looked at him with curiosity.

"We must go, sir. We won't fool them forever," said Runyon off to my left.

"No, you're quite right, Runyon. Can we have a hand with the luggage?" he asked me.

Dagon, the boy soldier and my Master at Arms, was the first to run to the sphere, pulling a suitcase from the top of the stack. Chineel and I followed. With Runyon carrying the last two until all the luggage was aboard.

"Come and see this," said Aristaeus, walking into the port bay. He threw several switches at the console, then turned to us, winked and returned to the console, speaking to the console.

"All right, Flax. Let's see you."

Aristaeus stood like a proud papa, with Runyon, Dagon, Chineel and me looking on. Flax raised her head over the console, then blinked twice. She smiled with delight, leaned forward and stepped out of the console. She took two steps forward and stood in the middle of our circle, surrounded by her crew. She wore a wide-skirted dress, buttoned to the throat and down to the wrists with snap-button gloves. She was the perfect lady for Victoriana.

"Wow!" said Dagon.

"Beautiful!" added Chineel.

"How far can she go?" I asked.

"It depends on what's in between. If there's nothing at all, even atmosphere, a long distance, thousands of miles. If there are planets and ships in the way, less. Out here, ship to ship, with all this atmosphere, I think ..."

A slight trembling under our feet returned us to the task at hand. Flax spoke.

"I'm still getting used to my sensors as you've set them up, but I think I can safely say that there are several spheres and a troop shuttle coming toward us at great speed."

"The CG boys," said Aristaeus.

Sure enough, a glance out of the port bay told the tale: three gleaming spheres like the one Aristaeus rode up on were coming down the roadway toward the sky port. Behind them, a hovercraft with three doors on each side rumbled toward us.

Flax started the landing thrusters as Runyon moved the sphere out of the way so as not to impede our takeoff. I reached inside the port bin for a blaster.

A hand reached out and held mine. It was Aristaeus.

"No, Star. If they see a blaster in your hand, they'll shoot to kill without hesitation."

"I won't be taken without a fight," I said, verging on the level of a threat, though he was not the target.

"I understand. Let's see if Flax can get us off the

ground first."

An explosion shook us, making me drop the blaster in order to get a hold on my surroundings. I picked up the weapon and dove for the bay door. The spheres carrying CG troops were dodging fire from above. The first had been knocked out and the second was showing damage on the starboard side. The troop carrier rocked on its mags as a blast pitted the ground two feet to one side. The troop carrier veered off to one side, hitting loose ground. The hovermags sent a cloud of dirt and debris into the air. The third sphere turned and drove off on a perpendicular path, trying to get as far from the source of the fire as possible.

High above our position, I saw a strange vessel descending upon us.

The vessel was easily five times the length of Exterra Bacchus and many times as tall, with landing thrusters fore and aft. Six gigantic cruising engines clung to its belly. High along the sides ran three rows of windows. Below the windows, three rows of gun ports. Two of the ports on our side were open. On the bow was a painted depiction of a tremendous serpent about to strike.

The vessel dropped onto the deck on our starboard side, with a clear shot at the CG troopers and a clear shot at us. Two of the big guns aimed directly at Flax.

"Pirates!" said Aristaeus.

The Holographic Captain

Two doors opened on the pirate vessel, One fore, one aft. From them stepped men wearing remnants of old military uniforms and armed for a war. The one closest to me flashed two pistols with a third stuck in his belt, available for a quick reach. The other had a sword in one hand and a blaster in the other, ready to fry me or gut me, whichever was easier. The large bay door opened to reveal three more standing in the shadows.

On the other side of the vessel, the guns continued to fire until at last there was silence. I wondered what was happening on the other side of the giant pirate vessel.

The man in the middle stepped out. He wore two guns,

one high on the waist and one low on his thigh.

He had his thumbs in his pants and looked at me like I was a menu item, sizing me up to order me or leave me on the serving table.

"I'm lookin' for the captain, Captain Bacchus." He looked down the line of us, from Aristaeus near the front to me aft. He waited only a moment, then continued. "Star-wort Bacchus. Captain of the vessel."

He paused at Runyon, looking him in the eye. Runyou didn't even blink.

"You Star-wort?"

Runyon slowly shook his head.

"C'mon now, don't be shy. Where's this captain, this Captain Bacchus?"

"I'm Captain Bacchus," said a voice behind me. There stood Flax, as tall as the pirate doing the asking and sporting a one piece leatherette unitard with a blaster on one hip and a five-inch blade on the other. Her hair was pulled back into a bun on the back of her head, ready for action. She stood prepared for a challenge, as if she and the pirate chief would fly at each other any second.

"You've led a lot of people on a merry chase, Captain. I have got to congratulate you on such a well-played game, but now it's got to come to an end, as all things must. I've got ..." The pirate chief looked up and down the row, counting "... five reasons you should consider telling me what I want to know sooner rather than later."

My heart stopped as the world went into slow motion. I didn't hear anything, but I did see the new holograph of Flax go into a crouch and reach for her blaster, which was as holographic as she was.

At that moment, a blast of blue fire came out of the sky, I could not see from where, and knocked the pirate chief off his feet and back into the bay. His men raised their weapons, unsure whether to just fire or wait for an order. A blast knocked the aft man off his feet and another cut the man at the forward hatch in half.

The two in the bay dragged their dazed captain further into the shadows as the bay door began to close. The aft man leaped into the door as the vessel rose into the air.

Two more shots from the unseen source rocked the pirate ship, no doubt giving the pirates a reason to grab onto something. The pirate vessel turned hard to starboard and soared off out of sight amid the fire and fury of the new vessel's landing thrusters.

As it lifted off, the scene on the road behind was revealed. One sphere had taken off, hightailing it out of sight before it could be fired upon; the other two were by the side of the road, completely destroyed. The troop carrier was on its side with smoke coming from the open gash across its side from front to back. No troopers were standing. The pirates had just saved us from Central

Government troopers, a meeting that rarely ends well.

In its place, a vessel almost the size of the pirate vessel, but better kept, landed and leveled its guns on our happy band. It was the third time we had been threatened with violence in the space of an hour.

The ship itself was gunmetal black with two central bay doors. Fore and aft of the bay doors were gun ports. The ship was wide with a high rear deck. I was happy it had not landed on top of us, for it would have crushed us all in a stroke.

High on the bow of the ship, the silvery wings of Icarus proclaimed the vessel to be of the Icarus Constabulary.

The main door opened to reveal none other than our old friend, Captain Vikare. With him was the young Sergeant Ariadne. Dagon blanched and looked at me. I believe he secretly hoped he would run into the young sergeant, but not like this.

Aristaeus, Runyon and Chineel waited to see how this would play out.

"Over to you, Captain," said Flax, as she faded into nothingness. Vikare and Ariadne both showed considerable surprise at the sudden disappearance of one of our party.

Behind me, I heard the thrusters powering down. The quiet that followed seemed eerie. I had almost gotten used to thrusters and cannon-fire as a backdrop to the day. Now, I hesitated to talk for fear my voice would sound as thunder and break the ears of those standing too close.

"Good to see you, Captain," said Vikare.

"And you, Captain. It hasn't been that long, you know. We just left Cecrops."

"Yes, I know, but then an alert showed up about a pirate ship by the name of Exterra Bacchus and we got all excited about seeing old friends."

"You mustn't take every alert that comes down the line at face value, Captain. Some of it is rubbish. Did a picture come with the alert?"

"Yes, but it looked more like the ship that just left than your Exterra. Speaking of which, what happened to your crew member, the young woman who was just standing here?"

"She had to go, she had work to do." I was trying to keep a straight face.

"I'd like to have a chat with her, if that's not too much trouble." Vikare and Ariadne moved a few steps closer, until they were closer to our vessel than their own. The feeling of tension lessened as we relaxed, though their vessel still had guns trained on us.

"We can go inside and talk. She's not used to being outside."

"We should do that, then. We do have a few

questions."

"Mi casa es su casa," I said, remembering a piece of vintage slang Flax taught me early in our relationship.

"Thank you, Captain." Vikare walked toward the open bay, followed by Ariadne.

"Captain," came a call from an external speaker on the constabulary vessel. "Sensors have picked up..." The rest of the message was lost beneath the earsplitting noise of thrusters powering up on both ships. The constabulary vessel immediately lifted off the ground.

"Inside," yelled a voice from inside my own bay. It was Flax, throwing protocol aside. With the thrusters already warmed, she lifted off immediately. The bay door closed with a slam, sending the visiting captain and sergeant to the bay floor. Exterra rocked back as she took off to avoid cannon fire.

On the bridge I saw a CG vessel many times larger than the one that brought Captain Vikare. It was firing at Vikare's ship as well as ours. Two dozen gun emplacements lined its sides and decks. The operations tower stood five stories high. The ground shook and everything was sent rolling, even the disabled CG vessels. On the bow, the mighty Central Government emblem of a gloved fist striking the ground glowed as if painted in lights.

"Could we go, Flax?" I said as Vikare settled into the

co-pilot's seat.

"Yes, Captain," came the reply.

Flax fired the thrusters at an odd angle, sending us in an unexpected direction. The CG ship fired but missed. Then it fired on the constabulary vessel and found its mark. The last thing we saw before leaving Victoriana was the vessel of the Icarus Constabulary exploding, going down in flames with all hands. Only two escaped the destruction of the Icarus vessel: Vikare and Ariadne were on board with us and, like it or not, were now part of our crew.

"Executing evasive moves, Captain," said Flax.

Captain Vikare looked at me, his eyes knitted. He knew that voice, it was the disappearing woman.

"Thank you, Flax."

Explosions from behind told us the CG vessel was still firing as we escaped. I thought I would take the chance to explain to Captain Vikare.

"The exterior platelets are changing to conform to the color and temperature of the far side of the vessel, making us invisible to all forms of detection, including direct human sight. Not that it is used anymore. We have, in essence, disappeared."

"Much like the woman who vanished earlier."

"Yes, Captain, much like her."

When blackness enveloped us and the Red Stroke

Drive kicked in, Ariadne slipped into the navigator's seat behind Vikare.

"Your orders, Captain?" said Ariadne.

Vikare looked at me. "You heard her: Your orders, Captain?"

Captain's Orders

"Flax, set sail for Khons, if you please."

"Aye Captain," came the reply.

"We'll have to make a stop between here and there, fuel and supplies," said Aristaeus over the intercom.

"I have evaluated the ship's fuel expenditures and food stores, adjusting for the extra crew members, and have made a reservation at a station. We'll be under a false name."

"Thank you, Flax," I replied, hearing Aristaeus make the same simultaneous reply.

"We can talk in the galley, Captain, Sergeant." I got up from the pilot's seat and took the pair through the bay to the galley. At the table sat Dagon and Chineel discussing our new crew additions. Runyon stood at the cooking station making tea. Chineel didn't look happy at seeing someone at her cooking station, but Runyon was a guest and Aristaeus had specific requests with regards to his tea.

"Where is Aristaeus?" I asked as I entered the galley.

"Head under the bonnet," said Dagon. "He's doing diagnostics on the upgrades recently added to Flax. I think he is doing more upgrades as we speak."

"Yes, we've already seen one of his upgrades. I have to admit, I trust him under her hood. Have a seat, Captain, Sergeant. Please let me begin by saying I am sorry about your crew. How many were aboard?"

"Three, brave constables all," said Sergeant Ariadne. I could tell she cared for them deeply. She struggled not to choke up and a tear was forming in her eyes.

"The Central Government crew must have thought our vessel was the pirate ship," added Captain Vikare.

"The Central Government doesn't care whose ship it was, Captain. It was there and not their ship, so they fired."

"Still, we have to report the loss."

"Yes, of course. As soon as we reach landfall at the station Flax has chosen, you will be let off to make your report. Naturally, you will be painted with the same brush they use to color the pirate ship, and us."

"They could not possibly confuse a Constabulary

vessel with a pirate ship!" said Ariadne, torn between grief and anger.

"Look around, Sergeant. Do you see a pirate vessel? Are there cannons at every port, firearms stacked in every corner or munitions hiding under the galley serving board?"

Ariadne did look around. Dagon was reading a slat regarding Earth history while Chineel worked on the food stores to determine what we needed to feed four extra crew members. Runyon was at the cook station making tea and wearing Chineel's apron. I sat calmly at the head of the table, unarmed and unthreatening.

"No, Captain, but there have been reports..."

"Flax," I called out.

"Yes, Star," Flax responded from the console.

"Please play us the CG reports of the encounter on Victoriana."

A flat, uncaring voice came from the console:

"Central Government Peacemakers on mission to bring order to the area were attacked without provocation in the lawless city of Victoriana. The attacker is believed to be the notorious pirate vessel, Exter Brackus. Lost in the violent and unprovoked attack were a Central Government vessel, a shuttle for CG Peacekeepers and eight unarmed Envoy Trans-globes. The battle began with the unilateral attack and destruction of a local constabulary vessel, which went down with all hands before a shot in defense could be fired. Thirty-five souls were lost. A Central Alert has been issued for the captain and crew of the pirate vessel Exbrackius."

"Now, Captain. Did they get any part of that right?" I asked.

"Only the location."

"Do you think you can say anything that will correct them?"

Captain Vikare gave a long, deep sigh. "No, they have it the way they want it. Of course, they couldn't get the name of the vessel right, or even uniform in the same broadcast."

"And no one will contradict them. The pirates certainly aren't calling in to correct the report. I believe you are listed among the dead. On Icarus, they'll be wondering where the other thirty crewmen came from."

"The CG is on Icarus by now," said Ariadne, lowering her voice and eyebrows.

"Then anyone who contradicts the official report will be considered treasonous. Are there any more questions?"

The galley was still. Even Runyon stopped stirring his tea. All looked at the Icarus Captain with expectation. He looked into the space between, then down, lowering his head once and then again.

"No, Captain. I believe you have covered it all. Thank you for bringing us aboard. I fear had we remained on the ground in Victoriana, we would be listed among the dead for certain."

"Yes, that is the case. There will be much crying, not only for those lost, but for the many lost in Victoriana. Indeed, for the loss of Victoriana, which was more than a city, it was a way of life, peaceful and gracious. Many were the times we considered making Victoriana our home."

"You must tell me about it," said Captain Vikare.

"Aristaeus will do the telling, and Runyon there. They know it far better than I. But I can tell you about Khons where we are bound and Bacchus, which is a farther destination. We keep hoping for a quiet, predictable journey without hair-raising stories to tell, but we have yet to experience that."

Chineel and Dagon looked at each other and grunted, rolling their eyes at my enormous understatement. The stories were about to come rolling out of them when Aristaeus entered, wiping grease from his hands with a cloth.

"Well, there is no damage and all systems seem to be working well. There are a few minor bugs yet, but nothing I can't work out on the way. How long until we reach landfall, Flax?"

"Three days Navtime. We should be out of provisions by then and will need to stock up. I have us at a safe station where we are not known and will not be suspected."

"That's just right. Thank you, Flax."

Flax had yet to make an appearance, though she is ubiquitous and with us always. Aristaeus sat down and received tea from Runyon.

"How many souls lost, Captain," Aristaeus said to Vikare.

"Three good men and true, Doctor. Thank you for asking."

"We've all lost much. We can lay down and cry ourselves to sleep or to death, or we can stand up and ... but I shouldn't be talking treason with a Constabulary Captain and his decorated Sergeant."

"Think of us as crewmates, Doctor. To say we are 'in the same boat' would be a vast understatement." Aristaeus smiled and took a sip of his tea.

"My own crew, save for Runyon there, is aboard a transport for the outer rim where friends and family are waiting to take them in. The outer planets have many problems to yet work out, but at least they are free to do so, as the Central Government has yet to plant an iron boot there. Our own Captain Starwort has lost her family and has few remaining friends she can count on. Chineel on your right has a similar tale until she was rescued by Star. Dagon is the last of a race that had known only war for centuries. He is the one living soldier of that conflict, a survivor of a dying planet. I suppose it is now dead, as planets go, and therefore, at last, at peace."

Dagon drew in a breath, stiffening his features. I once said the soldiers were children, but was corrected: the children were soldiers. Now they were gone and Pallas was without air or water, at peace for the first time in living memory.

"I am alive," Dagon said without stress or color. "The opposing side is not. I have won the war. All hail the conquering hero."

"So you see, Captain, there are tales to tell all around."

"Ares, which could be translated as god of war, but as we're all friends, please, call me Ares."

"Dione," said Sergeant Ariadne. "I was named after an obscure Greek goddess who, according to some legends, was the mother of Aphrodite. Ariadne is a corruption of Ariadna, the daughter of the king, Minos."

"Starwort," I added. "A plant growing in tidepools on Earth, signifying afterthought."

"Time for soup," said Chineel, smacking the table. She was not about to go into her name.

"Yes," said Dagon, not ready to play either. "I'm hungry. Who else is hungry?"

As Dagon and Chineel busied themselves at the counter, I leaned in to Dione and Ares. "Chineel was named for the Manchineel flower, signifying betrayal. I've never known anyone as loyal. People are rarely like their names suggest."

I leaned back, "And then there's Flax. You heard Flax speaking and saw her briefly. When I first came aboard I considered her my benefactor and still do. The flax flower means benefactor, so I called her Flax."

"There's one who is missing," said Ares, "Galium. Where is Galium?"

"Galium, named for a flower signifying rudeness, was never on Cecrops to be found. It was a false message sent by Crinole Gargon in an effort to lure Flax into her clutches."

"You proved to be too much for her."

"It would be unwise to underestimate us."

"And yet," added Aristaeus, "that continues to happen, time after time."

"Yes, people are so silly," I said, smiling and rocking back from the table.

The conversation lightened after that. Chineel brought food to the table and we sat, seven all at once.

I reflected that the Exterra class is set up for a crew of nine. We still had bunks for two more. I wondered if we would exceed our limit before the end of the trip.

Sleepless

I sat in the galley in my blue silk pajamas, barefoot in the corner side chair in the corner. I tucked my feet under me to keep them warm. Flax raised the temperature for me but respected my unspoken desire for privacy and solitude. She knew me better than anyone, except Abigail, my childhood friend.

The lights were down, only the glow from the console and the constant crew lights lining the walkways and hatches lit the galley, casting faint, nebulous shadows across the room.

Flax was walking about in full hologram, practicing, or maybe just enjoying being free of the console. I was reflecting on the turn of events that brought us here.

I was hoping to spend some time in Victoriana, laced in whalebone and crinoline with button shoes and a hat larger than any I had seen. There were drawbacks to the costuming, but they worked themselves out. On one hand, it was difficult to do just about anything in the gloves, which buttoned at the wrist and when paired with a sleeveless dress, went up past the elbows. On the other hand, as I was a lady, there wasn't much expected of me, so I just sat and folded one gloved hand over the other. It was a simpler time, a quieter time. It took some getting used to, but I was willing. The Central Government, of course, didn't care for it at all. People doing what they wanted made the CG nervous. Everyone had to be under their thumb and tightly controlled. To have people going around without implanted chips, thinking their own thoughts, responsible for their own finances, families, houses. It was unthinkable.

Flax was drifting from the bridge in her full form when a sound from the sleep chamber caught my attention. I was not the only one awake.

Captain Ares Vikare stumbled from the sleep chamber and into one of the galley seats. He had on a set of pajamas, presumably from Runyon, and bare feet as well. Perhaps he was also in the mood to consider the events that brought him here. Perhaps he was thinking of the three that were lost, the three that had become thirty-three in a Central Media report.

Ares looked up and froze as a silent figure drifted through the wall of the galley from the bay beyond. It was Flax in her Victoriana mode. She sported a full skirt, a blouse buttoned to the throat, full length gloves, wide hat with a gigantic feather and a lady's parasol. She drifted from the wall toward the center of the room and right through the galley table. As she passed, she turned toward Ares holding a gloved hand to her mouth; she extended the index finger and held it to her lips. She then drifted on feet that made no sound through the far wall into the sleep chamber.

Ares sat at the table transfixed. He had forgotten to breathe and was on the verge of passing out. I decided to disturb his reflections.

"She doesn't sleep," I said from the dark corner of the galley.

"Whoa!" cried Ares, jumping straight up and turning to me. He remembered how to breathe and held his chest, panting, with the other hand on the galley table. It was going to be a while before he spoke, so I just sat there until he got hold of himself.

As his breathing quieted and he returned more or less to normal, he sat down in a seat closer to me.

"You don't see that every day. I've never been on a haunted vessel before."

"I think every ship ought to come with one, just to keep the crew on their toes."

"So that is Flax."

"Yes, it is she. Her transformation has been epic. She began as the ship's computer. As I spoke to her, she spoke back. Soon we were in a conversation. She was already impressively developed when we met Doctor Genus. He went wild when they met. They held conversations long into the night, conversations I couldn't share, technically over my head."

"Will the Doctor take over now that he is aboard?"

"Aristaeus? No, certainly not. He is the gadgeteer, I am the Captain. Flax is the vessel and the computer. Aristaeus gave her a face and now a full form to ramble in, but she is the ship. How can the ship be the captain, or the captain be the ship? If I am arrogant enough to believe I could traverse this expanse, one step outside will correct the error in my thinking."

"Yes, even opening a window will do that out here."

"We all have our place. It is not by any grand design, but by natural adjustment. No one is given a place out here, you earn it. Sometimes you end up where you had not intended to go. Sometimes, in retrospect, where you went was where you were supposed to go in the first place. Prediction becomes difficult."

"I have experienced that in the past few hours. I didn't

come here to arrest you, you know."

"Oh?"

"No, I saw the alerts and knew they had to have it wrong. But the CG was at our doorstep and I needed a reason to go chasing pirates. I took Ariadne, as she is the sharpest of my junior officers. I chose three more. I'm sorry for their loss, but they would probably not prefer to be in Icarus right now. Where the CG steps, nothing grows thereafter."

We both stared into space, having nothing left to say about that.

Flax's ghostly appearance entered through the hatch from crew berthing. She was once again in the faux-leather unitard, buckled and belted, fixed for battle. Of course, it was all hologram, nothing real about it. She was stretching her wings.

"Pardon the intrusion. I have been trying out Aristaeus's new holographic body. I chose the crew's sleep time as I felt I might upset them if I wandered around Exterra at random."

"Yes, you well might. You gave Ares a start."

"Apologies, Ares. I will not suck your blood or eat your brain, I am a friendly ghost."

"Thank you, Flax. I'll keep that in mind."

Flax moved on, smiling at her joke. Ares was still recovering, but admired the technology.

"She has good control over the hologram."

"Shh!" I said. "Not so loud. She thinks she's real." Flax turned her head to regard me, pausing in her walk. Ares showed surprise at the playfulness between a captain and his ship, even if his ship appeared as a walking woman.

She had gone when Ares spoke again.

"I don't know what to do. When we get to the station, there will be fuel and supplies, and a way to send a message, I suppose, but what do I say? If I refute the Central Media report, I will be guilty of treason. If I even say my name, I will be considered... I don't know what. I'm dead, for Achilles sake. No one other than those aboard know that I am even alive."

"You have options. It's good to have options. If you are under the thumb of the CG, you have no options. If they say 'Blue is orange' that's the way it is."

"And if I return to Icarus?" asked Ares.

"If you return to Icarus, rejoicing at your escape from death will be short-lived as you will be taken into custody and charged. There are no heroes where the CG plants a foot."

"Then I have one option, to go with you to Khons. Where then, I don't know."

"You could capture a pirate ship and bring the crew under your heel. Together we could terrorize the outer rim like Anne Bonney and Edward Teach."

"Who?" The Captain looked totally lost in the reference.

"Edward Teach, Blackbeard. Famous pirate? Never heard of him? Don't you read?"

"Are they active in the outer rim?"

"No, they were active on Earth a few hundred years ago. They sailed in water-going ships and risked hanging daily. They are a very colorful part of Earth history. If you want interesting history, always look to the villains."

Night Crawlers

My smallish clothing told me I was not yet grown. My lack of higher education told me my schooling was unfinished. Yet I was the captain of a starship and called by some a pirate. I was a landowner with an entire planet among my holdings. But I was also a wanted criminal with a string of bodies in my wake. Whether or not it was known who killed them, whether or not I held the weapon or arranged events to the detriment of my foes, if you removed me from the equation, there would be more people in the world today. Of course, given that they were mad killers, my actions might have spared many lives.

I saved the life of my childhood friend, Daphne, when

we were attacked in the refresh room of the covered marketplace on Khons.

The man from the wedding party was put in the hospital after our chase through the Icarus streets in trash haulers, and killed there by another. Still, he would be free and walking the streets if not for me.

If there is a Heaven, if there is a Hell, I might not be slated for either without question. There could be a grand argument at the gates of either. I will probably need a lawyer.

I thought of Galium, who posed as my lawyer in Daedalus. Yes, he could be my lawyer, though he will be arguing just as hard for himself.

When tiredness weighed me down and sleep overtook me, I felt the most vulnerable. My fears were not being overcome by enemies, but by memories, memories that crawled through my dreams.

Such were the thoughts that lulled me to sleep between Victoriana and the refueling station.

It was not, however, angels or demons who came to visit in my slumbers, but my childhood friend, Abigail.

"Star, it is so good to see you! Isn't your dress pretty!"

I turned in place and saw a mirror behind me. The full-length, oval mirror had a wooden frame and sat upon the floor. In it I saw a girl of a dozen seasons in a yellow dress, tied with a bow at the waist. A matching ribbon bound back her soft, light-brown hair.

"It's Flax," I thought. "Flax as a young girl." But I knew it was me.

Turning again, I saw Abigail in a similar dress, hers of blue. She smiled at me and raised her hands, reaching to me.

I ran to my friend, with whom I had shared everything, every secret, and hugged her, tears streaming from my eyes. A deadly flu had swept our school and many of the tender young ladies succumbed to the illness. Abigail was among them.

"Oh, I have missed you."

"And I have missed you, sister. But you know I am always with you."

"I have done terrible things, sister. You would not want to know me as a grown woman."

"But you are not a grown woman, Star, you are still a girl and have been thrown into terrible circumstances time and again. You are still facing trials."

"I don't know what I would do without you, Abigail. You are my dearest friend."

"You have many friends, my darling Star. You need only look around you, they will stand by you. But the trials are not over, as I have said."

"You could always see more than most."

"Sush, sister! I see you in your father's house, but it is

not your father who is there, it is a friend who looks like your father. And it is not him either, but a representation of him. I see your friend, the friend from school."

"Daphne? She lives on Khons."

"Yes, it is her, but it is not. It is her mother. But it is her. She is her mother."

"That doesn't make sense," I said, surprised at hearing my own voice as a child.

"It's all I have, you're going to have to work with it," replied Abigail, her hands on her hips.

"Please don't scold me, sister. I have had a long day."

"Yes, you have. Attacked by soldiers of the Central Government, then by pirates, then by local authorities of another planet, then by the Central Government again. I don't know how you keep it all straight, Star."

"You know all of that?"

"I wouldn't have missed it! But listen close now, there is more to come."

In my heart I felt tired; I didn't want more to come. Abigail read my thoughts and feelings. She continued for my sake: "Silver globes attack you but a silver globe will save you. The child in your care will care for you as an adult. One prison is a playground and another prison is your shoe. Please don't ask me what that means. It makes no sense to me either."

"You are speaking in riddles and circles, sister."

"Yes, that's right, you should keep that in mind. The riddles are circles and the circles are riddles. That's very good, Star. You see? You are a bright girl! Now, what have you learned just recently? Recite your lessons."

"Look rather than think, know rather than guess. Do not run footraces with children. I am stronger and more powerful than I have ever been permitted to believe. I think that's correct."

Abigail kissed me on the cheek. She held both my hands.

"That's right, Star. You will touch many lives yet. And now..."

Abigail took me by the shoulders and began to shake me. She shook me harder and harder, as if she would shake me to pieces. I shut my eyes tight to withstand the shaking, but when I opened my eyes, it was not Abigail's girlish face I looked into, but Chineel's, framed by soft, red curls. She sat on the bed and had me by the shoulders.

"Wake up, sleepy-head. We're almost at the refueling station."

My Father's House

The refueling station was out of the way and just the bare bones. A fueling outlet and a small general store were the main part. There was nothing to see. The surveillance cameras were broken and the counter clerks didn't care. Nothing of interest ever happened at the station, so there was nothing to record or report.

Ares and Dione purchased clothing, as did Dagon, who was growing fast. He was no longer the boy soldier; he would soon be a man. Chineel and I tended to the ship's stores at the chandler shop.

"I was hoping for some fresh vegetables," said Chineel.

"If you see any, get them," I replied.

"Anything fresh?" she called out to the clerk.

"Every three weeks. It's been two."

"Get the stasis-packaged. It's likely to be your best bet," I warned her.

With ship's stores replenished and the register at full, we set off once again for Khons. I noted with some interest that Ares did not make a report of the events in Victoriana.

"So, no report, Captain?" I asked.

"No, Captain. I did not make a report. The truth would have, in this instance, made things worse. And you don't have to call me Captain. As far as I am concerned, you are the only captain that matters here. I am Ares Vikare, private citizen aboard a friend's vessel."

"As you wish, Citizen Vikare."

"No, that doesn't sound good either. Let's just go with Ares."

"Ares it is. You can call me Star."

"Star," said Flax from the console.

"Yes, Flax,"

"Please come forward, there is something different about Khons."

"On my way."

I went forward to the bridge, followed by Ares and Dagon. Ares tried for the co-pilot seat, but Dagon beat him to it and with his seniority aboard, Ares graciously let him have it. I looked out from the pilot's seat onto a town I knew well. It was evening and the lights should be on in house after house as darkness descended. How often had Daphne and I giggled until the daylight was gone, then turned on the lights and giggled for hours more. This was my home town.

"What do you see, Flax?"

"I want to know what you see, Star."

"I see the town of my youth, where my father and mother raised me until their deaths. My uncle's house was home for a short while, then the girl's academy. For a while I stayed with Daphne, my friend. Oh, yeah, and I killed a guy in the refresh room at the local shopping complex."

I could feel Ares and Dagon looking at me with some surprise, partly because of the news itself and partly the way I delivered it. My cavalier attitude toward the death of a man was of interest to them.

Neither knew what I was capable of when cornered, but they would treat me with a little more respect in future.

"But that's not what you asked. I see that it's growing dark and yet the houses have not turned on their lights. I see that one in three street lamps are on and they are dim. I see that there is a presence on the streets, silver globes such as the ones carrying the peacekeepers we recently encountered. They appear to be patrolling the streets."

I felt Flax cut the landing thrusters and engage the Gull Drive, named because it seemed as though the vessel was gliding on the currents like a seagull. The Gull Drive was silent and could not be detected by a heat signature or any other method of tracking. It was slower than thrusters and had a limited range, but it was what was needed now.

As darkness descended, so did Flax, down to just above the roofs of the houses.

"If you go down that street you will get to the school where I was incarcerated," I said, pointing to the right. "My uncle's house is not far, straight ahead."

Flax had coordinates delivered by Galium. She knew where she was going but still needed human eyes on the streets as we passed them.

"Yes, here it comes, up on the right. It should be right... here."

As Flax slowed, the lot containing my uncle's house appeared, but not the house. It was a burned out lot. The house itself was a cinder in the center. Nothing was left of my uncle or the house he lived in. I could feel Chineel over my shoulder. She looked out, said nothing and went back to the galley. She had been married to him and left just before I was sent to live there. She never asked how he died. I never said. We left it at that.

"OK, Flax, I've seen it."

"There is not enough room to land on the street. There is a school that is not far. I will land there. With the camouflage live, we should be invisible to most sensors."

"I'll prepare the Jumper," said Dagon, disappearing into the bay.

The ill-designed four-wheeled, inline speeder had earned itself the nickname "Jumper" as it tended to jump off the road unpredictably, to the detriment of the riders. Dagon had taken this one apart and put it back together with a lower center of gravity and a wider wheel-base. It was no longer a jumper, but we still called it that. Many a childhood nickname sticks to the holder long into adulthood. Galium still called me 'Little Wort,' though I have often asked him not to. Rude, like his flower, Galium delighted in stirring old ashes to flame.

I missed him.

No, I reminded myself, I missed the idea of him.

Stomping Grounds

Flax set down behind the school, where no prying eyes could see. She activated the camouflage so no sensors could detect us. When she opened the starboard bay door, Dagon rolled the Jumper out with me behind him and Chineel behind me.

Dione Ariadne wanted to come along. She looked strange in a skirt and blouse, with flat, slip-on shoes like a girl but with a pistol strapped to her waist.

"Just in case," she said. I couldn't argue. I knew that Dagon was armed, Chineel had a blade at the small of her back and I had a blade strapped to my thigh. We looked so innocent, but yet were deadly.

As we tore through the darkened streets of my

childhood stomping grounds, my attention was split.

On one hand, there was the surrounding landscape to take in. How was it the same? How did it differ? Who was out there as a friend, who as an enemy. And who, if appearing to be a friend, might turn to a betrayer?

On the other hand, I had to reflect that Dagon looked good in his new shirt. It did not pull at the arms and pucker at the waist. It fit him. He was growing. The young boy we picked up on Pallas, the planet no longer at war, was becoming a man before my very eyes. I hadn't noticed that his voice had dropped an octave and his sparring matches had become less choreographed and more of a fight for my life. The boy soldier was not a boy anymore.

"Here are the coordinates," said Dagon, as he pulled the Jumper up to the front of a house on a street with a wide curve.

"I know this house," I said looking up with wonder in my eyes. "This is the house of my childhood."

The stillness of the street was multiplied by the silence when Dagon shut off the Jumper. I stood on the walkway I had often run along going to or from my parents' house. It had been sold. New owners had taken over and made renovations. There was possibly nothing here that would seem familiar.

Dione stood at the door. She tried the latch. It was

locked.

Dagon nudged her aside and worked the lock for a moment. A moment was all he needed; the door opened freely for him. As he held out a hand for Dione to enter before him, like a gentleman, she looked at him with curiosity in her eyes. She had been a constable long enough to know you don't pick a lock that fast without practice.

Inside it was completely dark, but our eyes soon adjusted, revealing a house devoid of furniture. There was not a seat or a table in the main room. There was no large table in the dining room and the bedrooms were empty save for one: the master bedroom was sparsely decorated with a double bed and a side table. The closet was empty. On the side table was a small box with a red button on the top. The words, "Press Here" were written on a piece of paper held down at the corner by the box.

"Step back," I whispered to my three companions. If it was a bomb or a trap, I wanted the damage contained.

I pressed the red button. A stream of light came from the box and shown on the wall opposite the bed.

It was Papa Posey, old when I knew him in Sterope, older now on the wall of my father's bedroom.

"Hello, Child. I had to make my escape and accepted a ride, but do not know the final destination. Find Jessamine, she will know where I am. She has been taken. They have her, but she is probably well cared for. She has been incarcerated at a most strange prison. It is 'The Dark,' which is merely a short name for 'The Dark Side of the Moon,' a resort on the far side of Earth's moon, which they call, oddly enough, The Moon. The unseen side is called the dark side, though it gets as much light as the other, I suppose. Go to 'The Dark Side of the Moon.' Find Jessamine. 'The Dark' has yet to experience a jailbreak. Can you guess why? Who would break out of a resort? Tell her the hot oil rubs and flowery drinks are all good and well but she has to go now. She'll know my location."

A voice sounded in the background. Papa Posey turned for a moment then back.

"I must go. I hope to see you all soon."

The message flickered. In the box on the table, a chemical reaction took place and a puff of smoke rose from within the box. The red button caught fire and burned with a blue flame.

Outside, a tumult caught my ear. Chineel was at the door.

"Khons Guard backed by CG forces are on the front lawn. We have to go."

From the old family room off the back yard I saw Chineel and Dione on the back lawn. I ran out to meet them.

"Where is Dagon?"

"He slipped out unseen. We don't know where he went," said Chineel.

"He's abandoned us!" said Dione with fear in her eyes.

"That would never happen!" I said.

A silver globe like the ones we saw on Victoriana hovered across the ground behind the house and up to the door where I stood. The driver's door opened, up like a bird's wing. There was Dagon in the driver's seat.

"It's not unlike a speeder. Get in, we've got to get out of here."

Dagon opened all the doors. Dione got in behind Dagon. I heard her say, "Sorry. I misjudged you."

A blast hit the ground between me and the sphere. The explosion knocked me backwards, unconscious.

Dazed, I lay on the ground where I played as a child. Soldiers stood around me. One helped me up.

"Who is she?" asked one of the Khons Guard officers.

"Be-demoned if I know. A Neighbor perhaps? Are you alright miss?"

The faces swirled around me, but I reached out and grasped a semblance of reality.

"Yes, I think so. I was talking to a Guard member and there was an explosion."

"The CG troopers are shooting at anything that moves. It's a wonder you weren't killed."

Two Khons officers helped me up, dusted me off and tried to put a smile on my face with reassuring phrases. There was no sign of Dagon or the sphere.

"Thank you, gentlemen. I was on my way to my friend's house when I thought I saw a light. I'll know better than to investigate such things in future."

"Yes, miss. You must take more care. The troopers believe there are pirates in the area."

"Pirates!" I said, trying to look surprised. "Oh, my! I'd best hurry on to my friend's house."

I scurried around the far side of the house and down a connecting path to Daphne's house three doors down the street. There was a dim light in the parlor; someone was home.

At the door, I tapped lightly. The Guard was three doors away and the CG troopers were backing them up, just itching to take over at the first opportunity.

I knocked again, a little stronger this time. The door opened and there stood Daphne's mother, looking at me with a disapproving look as usual.

"Hello, Star," said a familiar voice. It was not Daphne's mother, it was Daphne. In the dim hall light and dressed in a full frock, she took on the appearance of her mother, especially with her hair tied behind.

"Daphne?" I said, a little too surprised.

"What's wrong, Star, too full of yourself to recognize a

friend from school? You certainly don't mind stirring up trouble in your old neighborhood. The Khons Guard is searching the streets for a pirate and the description is of you. Don't think I didn't put together the events at the Khons Plaza. Three men dead and you in the middle of it. You were a bad seed then and you're a bad seed now."

"Daphne, what's gotten into you?"

"I woke up, Star. I found my place." It was an accusation rather than a statement.

"You turned into your mother!" I shot back.

"What's wrong with that? She lived a good and happy life. The only one who tried to take me away from following in her steps was you. Now the Guard is looking for you. I knew it would come to this, Star. I'm calling them."

Daphne closed the door. I couldn't believe my eyes. It was her and yet it was not, just like Abigail had said. It made sense now.

A CG trooper sphere hovered slowly down the curved street, a light shining on all the doors and windows as it passed. Another came right behind it. Behind that one, another trailed.

As the third sphere pulled up to the house, it slowed and the rear door opened. Inside was Dione waving a hand to me. I ran to the sphere and jumped inside.

"Where have you been?" asked Dagon.

"I met an old friend," I replied.

Dagon pulled forward to catch up with the other two spheres, then slowed to a crawl guiding the sphere into the line with the others. He drifted onto a side street and made a wide circuit of the houses, trying to avoid suspicion from the other spheres. Back in front of Daphne's house, he moved the sphere down the street at half speed. No one noticed. We were just another sphere, looking for anything out of the ordinary.

A block away, the blare of sirens broke the stillness and pandemonium broke loose. A half-dozen spheres came toward us with blue and red lights blinking and swirling from the top. Daphne's alarm had alerted them.

"Come with us," said a voice over the speaker on the console. Dagon turned around and followed.

We rode past my father's house to see Dagon's speeder in the front yard. A dozen CG troopers stood at guard, surrounding his speeder as if it would escape on its own.

"If we run, they'll chase us. This way, we're just another sphere, looking for the riders of that speeder." Dagon looked into the rear-view screen one last time at his beloved speeder. "But I'm keeping this sphere."

At the school, twenty spheres had assembled to aid in the search. Dagon slid by the lead row and around to the back of the school. Flax waited, invisible to all who did not know what to look for. Dagon brought the sphere up to the port bay. Flax opened the bay door so Dagon could bring the sphere inside. Flax started the Gull Drive and lifted off the ground as a platoon of CG Troopers double-timed into the yard.

Flax skimmed the trees until she was clear of town, then angled up toward the black sky above. She waited until she had cleared the atmosphere before engaging the thrusters. A minute and a half later, she cut thrusters in favor of the Red Stroke Drive. By the time Dagon had the sphere tied down, we were on our way with Khons in our rear-view screens.

The Dark Side of the Moon

At an exclusive resort named "The Dark Side of the Moon" suspected political prisoners were kept against their will but in extreme comfort and luxury. No one had ever escaped.

Jessamine, the girl from my childhood past in Sterope, sighed heavily, lying on a raised bed, covered with a soft, terry cloth sheet. There were cold, soothing pads on her eyes. At the end of the bed, a boy of tender years softly massaged her feet. Jessamine moaned like a young lover beneath his touch.

"Yes, it is wonderful," said the woman on the next table. "We should get drinks after this. Don't you think?"

"Definitely," replied Jessamine.

Later, reclining in the bar while strong young men dressed only in shorts brought them drinks in tall glasses, the woman reached out a hand.

"Semi. It's for Semiramis, but who wants to say all that? Just Semi will do."

"Jessamine," said Jessamine, taking the woman's hand.

Both women returned to their drinks, wrapped in soft robes and wearing sunshades against the strong light of the lunar day.

"Well, Jessamine, if we have to be held captive, I can think of worse places."

"Yes, this was a surprise to me. My one fear is that they will lose interest in me and ship me off to somewhere less attractive."

"Don't think about that. What do they want of you?" Semi reached into her bag and pressed a button on the side of her makeup case. As she sat back, Jessamine told her what they wanted to know.

"They want to know about a fellow I used to know many seasons ago. I haven't heard from him in such a long time, but they seem to think we're close. Also, there are some pirates allegedly running around in a renovated repair vessel. I haven't a clue what that's about."

"You don't know them?"

"No! I live quietly on Khons with my uncle Poseidon. We call him Papa Posey. He is the best cook! You should have his Universal Gumbo. One spoonful and you taste a dozen savory seafoods all at once. He uses exotic and plain fishes from several planets. It's amazing!"

"What fellow you used to know?" said Semi, bringing the conversation back to the reason for her being there. If she didn't get the information in the allotted time, she would be reassigned to somewhere less enjoyable.

"Those were wilder days! It was hard to tell the pirates from the poets. This one acted like a pirate but he was a poet. Galium was his name. It's the name of a flower signifying rudeness. It was an apt name for him; he had his rude side, for sure."

"Sounds colorful. You said those were wilder days. So what's he like lately?"

"I don't know. I haven't seen him since those days at the Mithra Tavern in Sterope. It got to be a popular place and we left when the tourists came in. I hear it's really gone downhill. The tavern is a diner now, where they serve overpriced snacks for rich people looking for a real experience. Ha! Real experience. As if..."

"Yes, yes. What about the pirates? You said you couldn't tell the pirates from the poets. So there were pirates?"

"Oh, no, not real pirates, just people who liked to think they were dangerous and colorful. There was one red-bearded man who had a young girl who followed him around all the time. He had this speeder he loved, but he hit the girl one day and she left him. Stole his speeder and left him. They never found the speeder."

"Was he one of the pirates on the repair vessel?"

"I have no idea. I don't know anything about a repair vessel. But I don't think he was a pirate, he was just mean and colorful and liked to think of himself as dangerous. Like so many guys back then. You know how it is."

"But the girl stole his speeder."

Jessamine sighed deeply, raised her sunshades and looked around. "Yes, she said it wasn't right to hit girls. Where is the boy with the drinks?"

Semi reached down to her bag and pressed the button again. She would get nothing from this woman today but useless reminiscences about old friends who were pretend pirates, poets trying to impress the girls.

"Too bad you don't remember. They might reward you if you remembered."

"Could be. The thing is, I have no idea who they're talking about most of the time."

Two guards appeared from the side room. They walked up to Jessamine and took hold of her.

"She says she doesn't know anything about Galium or the vessel. I believe her. This is a waste of time. Take her to the interrogation chamber."

At the interrogation chamber, the mood changed. Semi came in and sat on a hard chair across from Jessamine, who was also placed on a hard chair.

"I'm afraid the boy with the drinks won't be showing up. It's time you remembered what you know about a vessel known as Exterra Bacchus and her crew of pirates. There is Starwort Bacchus, a woman named Manchineel and an unnamed boy. The pirate Bacchus recently fled Icarus. Pursued by an Icarus vessel, she destroyed the constabulary ship with all hands at Victoriana. Many Central Government ships and personnel carriers were destroyed in the process."

Semi took out three photos, one of a dark-haired woman in a low-cut blouse, one of a youngish woman with bright red hair and one of a large pirate vessel bristling with guns. The vessel was clearly not Exterra class, which tended to be small and without armaments.

"Does this shake your memory?" asked Semi.

"I don't know her, or her, or that ship."

"What about this man?" Semi pulled a photo of a young man, bearded and smiling, but blurred and grainy as it was taken from a great distance.

"That could be Galium as I remember him. But I

haven't seen him since those days. I don't know where he is now."

"Do you remember that you expressed a fear that if you did not remember the information asked of you, a transfer to a less pleasant place might be your fate? Well, the moment for that transfer has arrived. The rubdowns and exotic drinks are over, Jessamine. From now on, inflicted pain will be the order of the day and it will grow worse as you continue to refuse to cooperate."

Semi stood and walked to the door. A guard opened the door. As she stepped out, Semi instructed the guard.

"Get her a course tunic and cut the lights. I'll be back tomorrow to continue questioning her."

Palace Guards

"It is a long way to Earth, Star. Are you sure she will be there when we arrive?"

"I don't have any other information, Flax. If we don't go and get her, we're at a dead end."

"I could send out a coded missive for Galium."

"No, don't involve him. He said he was going where he didn't want us to know. Let him go."

"There is something new you should know about Earth. It is surrounded by a security system larger than I have ever encountered."

I sat on the bridge holding my clarinet. I had yet to

play it within earshot of our new passengers and felt self-conscious. If I closed the door, I would raise suspicion, so I just held the instrument until my courage returned.

Flax raised her holographic head from the console as she did before Aristaeus programmed in a complete body. She liked her full-frame body, but didn't use it all the time. I suppose she was afraid she would wear it out. I didn't ask; there were other things on my mind.

"What is the security system like?" I asked.

"They are called Palace Guards, a ring of space mines surrounding the planet, not only equatorial, but to the north and south as well. There is no approach to the planet that is not mined. They connect in such a way that if you tried to fly between them, mines on all sides would explode, taking you with them. They are not rigged to capture vessels but to dispose of them if they try get through the net, which is against the law."

"I suppose it saves a lot of money on courts and trials and such."

"Yes, and incarceration. You can't lock up prisoners who are exploded into space dust."

"And you don't have to feed them, either."

"Yes. That's true. The savings would be considerable."

Flax and I sat looking at the stars flickering in the distance. With the Red Stroke Drive at cruise setting, we were traveling at speeds I only read of as a child. The stars that flew at us were in fact stationary, it was Flax who was moving so fast.

"Of course, there's the cost of replacing the mine once it had exploded," said Flax.

A light went on in my head.

"What about meteorites, Flax? Do meteorites ever set off mines?"

"I will check." There was a moment's flicker of Flax's holographic head as her attention was diverted. Then she came back. "Yes. It is a common occurrence. A meteorite that would otherwise burn up in the atmosphere of Earth would explode when hitting a mine. Therefore, the ring also protects the moon, which is without atmosphere. Once detonated, the mine would have to be replaced, the hole in the system repaired."

Flax turned toward me. She looked as if she were thinking, just coming upon a concept she had not considered before. She continued, still thinking.

"Of course, when a meteorite strikes a mine in the ring, there is an explosion and the meteorite blows up. A vessel is dispatched to replace the mine and reconnect it to the other mines. I doubt it would be a daily occurrence or even common, but not unheard of."

"Flax, as we approach Earth, check the system and see if any of the mines are blown and need replacing. We might be able to slip in before the repair can be made."

"I will begin checking as soon as we come within range."

I sat back, put the clarinet to my lips and played a few notes. This might be workable after all.

Pytho

"Track that vessel!" scowled Pytho.

"Scanning the immediate planets and trade routes, Captain. No sign of her so far."

Captain Pytho of the Free Vessel Kraken adjusted the sling that held his arm, the one that was broken when he was thrown back into his own bay by a blast from an approaching vessel.

"Just when I had her in my hands!" he muttered to himself.

The Free Vessel Exterra Bacchus was the same as his own, unaffiliated. Unaffiliated vessels were known, in his circle, as Free Vessels. It was another way of saying Pirate Ship. Everyone knew what you meant when you said it. There was no subterfuge, no attempt to cover the truth. Unaffiliated vessels belonged to no one but themselves. The Central Government in particular hated that concept.

Pytho looked at both doors to his master quarters. Once convinced he was alone, he brought a child's toy from his desk. It was a replica of a speeder, a four seater, though faded and old. Such replicas were no longer made, the plastic it took was too expensive these days. The cost would have been prohibitive for a toy. But this was not a new toy, but an old one.

On the bottom, written in a child's scrawl, was a single name: Horace. It had been his name as a child. His mother and father had named him after a famous poet of Earth's history.

It had been a long time since he had played with this toy on the carpet at his parent's home. He was happy then. He had many friends and his parents were well-off. Not rich by any stretch of the imagination, but able to buy him whatever he wanted, to provide his every need and most of his wants, which were many. Young Horace was the center of his universe. He was happy.

Then the agents of the Central Government came and took him. He had done nothing wrong, he knew, but his parents were the ones they were after. They had also done nothing wrong, but they had been suspected, then implicated, and then accused. Charges were filed and the parents of young Horace were taken and questioned. They died in questioning just as it was discovered that they were not the people who should have been named in the warrants. The names were similar and the street was in the same neighborhood. Someone's head would roll for this mistake. Horace, however, would be taken to the Custody Care Center. As a ward of the CCC, he would be raised as all the other children were raised, the children of the criminals of the state, those who broke the laws of the Central Government.

When pirates came to steal away the children, it was the parents of the children who came to take them. The CG said they were criminals and so criminals they became. Now they had come to steal their children. On the pirate ship, the Free Vessel Hades, named for the god of the underworld, he learned that the work was hard and the comforts were few, but he was free, no longer affiliated with the Central Government.

A light flashed at the door, indicating someone was there wanting to gain entrance. He returned the speeder to his desk and touched a blue dot on the screen to his left. The door clicked to unlock. When it opened, the first mate looked in.

"Captain, we've found the Exterra, headed for Earth."

"Now, why in the name of Zeus would they go to Earth?"

The Ceberus

As we flew at Red Stroke speed toward the hub of our universe, the central planet of Earth, the fueling station we had just left was visited by another vessel: The Ceberus, a cruising vessel of the Central Government of Earth. It had been called to check the route presumably taken by a sought-after pirate ship.

Vessels the size of the Ceberus did not land at the refueling station, but pulled up along side and docked at the refueling ramp. Rarely did the crew come ashore or into the general store. Never before had they come in armed and in strength. The counter boy looked up to see twenty armed troopers enter his tiny shop. They all looked the same with their faceplates down and their insignia covered. He could not know that the one who spoke to him was a Captain of the Guard.

"Exterra Bacchus," said the metallic voice, holding up a reader with a picture of a vessel also too large to dock and boasting guns at every port.

"Uh, uh, uh, No sir, not seen it. Nothin' like that has been here."

The picture flickered, changing to that of a pretty gypsy woman with black hair and large earrings. The Captain of the Guard pushed it into the boy's face.

"Bacchus! Seen her?"

"N-no, sir. She don't look familiar at all."

"They came this way."

"That woman, that vessel, never here. I promise you, they weren't here."

"Check your logs, who refueled? Who bought? Where is your security record?"

"Uh, Yes, sir." The boy began a search using an outdated screen and record locator. It was slower than the Captain was used to.

"Hurry up, if you want to keep your station."

"Hurrying, sir. There is no security record, the cameras have been broken for two nav-cycles, broken by marauders. But here, two constables and a boy came in to buy clothing. At the same time, two women purchased food stores. They paid in cash, some copper but mostly Universals. Their ship wasn't as big as that one and the woman wasn't like her, the one in the picture. One was red haired and her daughter had brownish hair. The vessel filled up, but it was much smaller than that one and had no guns on it."

"Where was it bound, this ship with no guns?"

"For the home system, Red Stroke speed all the way."

"Red Stroke Speed?"

"Yes, sir, the red-headed gal said they would 'Red-Stroke all the way home."

"And home is..." pressed the Captain.

"Can't say, they were headed for the central planets; Earth or Mars or the Meteor Belt. Hard to say."

"They didn't say?"

"No, sir. Didn't say."

The Captain of the Guard turned on his heel and strode to the door. As he went out, he gave one final order.

"Burn it!"

Commander Belus

On the Ceberus, Commander Belus glanced at the rear screen to see the fueling station exploding in stages as the charges they set reached the tanks, one by one. Besides the clerk there were five workers at the station. None of them claimed to know anything about the ship that stopped and filled their registers at the tanks or the people who purchased clothing and food from the general store.

"Everybody knows something," Commander Belus reassured himself. "Those who lie are hiding something. Those who refuse to answer when questioned deserve to die."

The family Belus referred to the old Babylonian name meaning the Lord. Commander Belus took this as a divine mission. Those who did not comply did not continue in life. He was the weapon that swept all offenders from the field.

"Where is that vessel?" boomed the Commander. Those near to him winced at the thunder of his voice.

"It was coming this way, but it is unsure if it meant to stop at the station. It is going along a route directly to the core, to Earth. He could be targeting Mars or the Meteor Ring, but it appears to be Earth."

"You are certain it is the vessel, Bacchus?"

"It appears to be larger than an Exterra class vessel, but it did leave Victoriana shortly after the battle there. It made an escape from our ship."

"Heh! Which is more than the Icarus Constabulary Vessel did. Local authorities out of their jurisdiction! They should know better! They won't make such a mistake again."

"They won't make any mistake again," quipped one trooper to the man next to him.

"And that is the lesson to be learned. Cross the Central Government and you don't get a second chance. Are you looking for a second chance, trooper?"

"No, sir."

"Then in the name of Baal, shut up!"

"Yes sir." The trooper gulped hard and made himself a promise not to speak again.

Belus looked at the big screen, at the vastness of space before him. He considered that he owned it, he owned it all. It was his from Souro Station, the space station circling Earth, to the furthest reaches of space where civilization has yet to set a foot. It was all his. Any who trespassed in his space would be punished by him, Commander Belus, The Lord.

"Sir, there is something here. It's probably nothing."

"Then tell me nothing, Amun."

The engineer expanded the 8th quadrant of the screen and the 8th again, showing a dot that could be anything or nothing.

"It could be a star, or a moon, or a bit of debris, but it is putting out a signal. It is a weak signal and is aimed toward Earth, or rather toward the controller station for that sector. It is unclear what the signal means, or if it really is a signal or just an anomaly."

"Keep on it, Amun. If it turns into something, let me know."

"Yes sir. Did you want to know about the larger ship as well?"

"Larger ship? This is the first I've heard. Speak, man!"

"Oh, well, there is a larger ship, that is, it is also just a dot, but appears to be on the same trajectory as the smaller one."

Amun brought the screen back and focused in on

another quadrant, expanding it three times until another dot held the center of the screen.

"It is a Drake class vessel, heavily armed and is sending out many signals in all directions. I can tell nothing more about it, but it is on a trajectory from Victoriana to Earth, without a stop at the refueling station."

"No one will be stopping at the refueling station any more, Amun. Keep an eye on the vessel. It is most likely the one we are looking for, Bacchus and its crew of cutthroats. Let me know if there is any change."

"Yes, Sir!" Ensign Amun snapped to attention. He had two ships in his screens and would track both of them to the ends of space if need be rather than let Belus down.

Dungeon

Deep in the depths of the labyrinth of tunnels bored into the cold, lifeless rock of Earth's moon, far beneath the lavish spa known as The Dark Side of the Moon, Jessamine sat in blackness to which she could not accustom her eyes, through which she could not see.

She was thirsty and hungry. The swill they brought her was undrinkable. It was all they brought. She was also tired, as she was afraid to sleep, not knowing what was in the cell with her, who might come in or whether she might wake up screaming - or not at all.

And she was dirty. She knew it. She could smell that she was dirty. There was no refresh area, just an indentation in the corner that she dared not investigate further. No bowl for water, no water if there was a bowl. She had gone from the best place she had ever been to the worst place she had ever been.

It might have been weeks, or hours, but it was probably days, when she nodded off to sleep in the middle of the room on the cold stone, no blanket and no pillow.

"Hey!" said a voice from miles away. "Hey! Wake up. I've brought you something."

Jessamine raised her head. There was light coming from the door. A guard stood in the doorway looking mean. Closer to her was a face, a pretty face framed by dark, curly hair.

"I'm Sirina. Well, actually, it's Aysu, but they want me to go by Sirina. It's more exotic for the men."

Jessamine tried to speak, but her mouth was dried shut. Aysu held a cup to her lips.

"Slowly at first. There you go, sweetie. I usually dance upstairs; I'm not much good at anything else. When I'm not dancing, they have me delivering water and something that passes for food down here. I can't say it's very inviting, but that's OK because it's not very filling either. That's it, have a little more of the water."

Aysu held Jessamine's face to the light. She twisted her mouth and knitted her brow.

"Listen, sweetie. They'll let you back up if you give

102.

them something. Tell them what you know. You'll be cleaned up and back in the spa in no time. Maybe I'll even get to dance for you, though it's mostly for the men."

Aysu rolled her eyes, her mouth twisted to one side. Then she got a different look and lowered her voice.

"Tell them anything, the wilder the better. It doesn't matter if you don't know anything. Just tell them something. Think back to the most unlikely person you can think of and tell them that he is a criminal mastermind who's got everyone fooled. They'll let you back up and you'll be fed and clean and we'll be friends."

"You done?" came a gruff voice from the doorway.

"Yes, sir, all done. Here I come." But she turned back to Jessamine before she left. "Oh! I know. A commander named Belus came for a visit and had me dance for him. He had a junior office who followed him everywhere, an Ensign Amun. They left for the far reaches. Tell them that Amun is someone's contact, the traitor, a mole even. It will take them forever to confirm the story but they'll know right away that he does exist. See you soon."

The girl got up and walked out of the door into the hallway beyond. She was bowed as she passed by the guard. The door was slammed shut and Jessamine was in the dark again.

Perfect Balance

I woke up not knowing how long I had been asleep. In the vastness of space it didn't much matter; that I got sleep at all was a good thing. I had no dreams, no forecasts and no premonitions - just sleep.

In the galley, former Constabulary Captain Ares Vikare sat at the big table. He was dressed in Runyon's pajamas. His feet were bare. I wore my dark blue pajamas and had found my slippers, so I was spared cold feet. Flax must have sensed Ares's cold feet, there was a warm flow of air across the floor of the galley.

"You couldn't sleep either?" asked Ares as I walked in.

"For all we know it might be morning, time to get up. I think I slept enough. Did you make morning ale?"

"No, I don't know my way around the galley. I don't want to step on Chineel's toes."

"She is protective of her galley."

"So, she's your cook and Dagon's your mechanic? Is that how it goes?"

"Chineel is my friend, so is Dagon. We are a family. We do what is needed. I'm not bad at a cook station, but she's better, so she took on the galley. Dagon is fascinated by things that go fast, so he took over the starboard bay as a workshop. He gave the speeder a wider wheelbase and lowered the center of gravity for greater stability on the road. It's a shame we had to leave it behind on Khons."

"But you gained a sphere. That should be some consequence to him."

"It will be, once he has taken it apart and put it back together."

Ares sat quietly. The man named for the Greek god of war was quiet and reflective. He sighed. His restless eyes couldn't land on anything but drifted around the galley.

"I know that feeling. You've lost everything and you don't know where to hang your hat, if you have a hat."

"Days, just a few days, so much has changed. It's not yet a week back in Icarus since I left. Sergeant Phaeton is probably saying to himself, 'The Captain must be having one grand time rollicking around in space.' When word comes home to them that the vessel was lost with all hands, they'll think I'm dead. And they'll believe you are the cause."

"Yes, the Central Media will certainly blame me for your untimely demise. They take a situation, decide how it can be worse and say it that way. Anyone who contradicts them disappears and is never heard from again."

"One day, I'm a captain of the Icarus constabulary, with a uniform and a medal, several medals in fact, and soldiers who snapped to when I spoke. Now I'm dead."

"Only you're not, Ares, you're sitting here alive."

"To what end? I know Sergeant Ariadne feels the same way. I mean Dione. I'm sure she misses the life she had just yesterday."

"I understand, Ares, I really do. There are things you come to lean on. You get up and put on your uniform and you know who you are. You put on your insignia and you know where you fit. You put on your medals and you know you've done well. But they are just things to lean on. Believe me, when I woke up this morning, once I had really woken up, I knew who I was, where I fit and that, all things considered, I have done well."

Ares looked at me, hoping my words would take on

meaning.

"Where do I go from here?"

"For now, you follow your captain. That would be me, incidentally. You'll go with me to release Jessamine from a prison she doesn't want to escape from. Then you'll go where she indicates to find Papa Posie. He will unravel the riddle and show us the key to Planet Bacchus."

"Then what?"

"You expect a lot for a little, don't you! I don't know, Ares! I don't have a crystal ball here, just my best guess. You can pick up a bride along the way and start a family on Bacchus. How does that sound?"

Ares drew a large mouthful of air, looked away and scrunched his mouth up. He was thinking about it.

"That's the second utterly fantastic future you have suggested to me. Both seem within the realm of possibility now. What a strange feeling."

"What? Being in charge of your own decisions? Making up your mind what will happen and then making it happen? Having a field of options and picking the one you want rather than living with the one you are handed? Yes, it is a strange feeling. Imagine how Flax feels."

"Flax? Your ghostly lady?"

"Yes, perhaps it's time you officially met the other woman in my life. Flax?"

A holographic head rose up from the console on the far

wall. I turned to speak to her.

"Would you care to join us?" "I would be pleased to, Star."

Flax stepped out of the console, as tall as the captain and dressed in pajamas and slippers. She walked to the galley table and sat in the chair next to me. She smiled at Ares and then to me, waiting for a question.

"Tell Ares your story, Flax."

I got up to fix morning ale for two as I listened to the familiar tale of the retrofitting of a repair vehicle to automation, adding an advanced computer salvaged from a much larger vessel. I felt a thrill to hear of the day a waif, a ragamuffin from the streets, tumbled into the bay while running from the landlord. I named her Flax, as she was my benefactor. We began to talk and in time, became friends. Doctor Genus added a holographic head, giving expression and a face to the advanced brain inside, a brain that was now extrapolating potential outcomes based on existing data and calculations, but with a touch of intuition as well. It had become a "she" and was now one of the crew, so much so that a clarification was in order. I cut into the conversation.

"We make a distinction these days between Flax and the vessel, Exterra. They were once inseparable but now, with this new innovation, she can leave the ship. They are no longer one entity."

"It is a strange sensation," said Flax.

"I expect so," replied Ares.

"You know, Ares, if I make an observation, Star suggested in passing that you take over the pirate vessel and bring the crew under your orders. You know it is not a bad suggestion at all."

"You heard that?" said Ares in surprise.

"Don't let the ears fool you. They are a holographic representation and do not actually hear. I am all over the vessel, inside and out; ubiquitous, as Star says. I hear everything. You might as well get used to that, because it is not going to change."

"I understand. Thank you. And how do you suggest I take over the pirate vessel?"

"If you have to be told how to do it, Captain, perhaps you are not the man for the job. I'll be keeping an eye on the charts, Star. Call me if you need me."

"Will do, Flax." I smiled. Flax might say she is on the bridge, but she just finished telling us she was all over the vessel.

She stood up and turned with a flare toward the console, but she faded before she arrived at the wall; simply vanished into air.

"She does have style," said Ares.

"Yes, she does. And she also has a point. You were the Captain of the Icarus Constables. You had fifty or sixty men and women under your command. You did not hesitate to fly into the teeth of the most dangerous enemy the planet had and yet to calmly question those who might be law keepers or might be law breakers. To find the pirate vessel, confront its captain, best him, win over the crew and take the whole thing back into the darkness to find your fortune is just the outline of the plan. The rest is logistics."

Spilling the Beans

Jessamine sat in a warm, comfortable room dressed in a soft robe and cozy slippers. She had been scrubbed and oiled, pampered and primped until she once again felt like a lady at a spa.

The woman known as Semi, for Semiramis, walked in similarly dressed with a smile and a tray of tea and cakes.

"There now, we can get comfortable and get this nasty business out of the way." Semi put the tray on the table between them and sat down, arranging herself for the interview.

There was no need for her to indicate or start a recording as everything within the room was recorded from the time anyone walked into the room and did not stop until the room was cleared.

"I don't know why I didn't think of it before, all those names must have just slipped my mind. But you know the more I thought about it..."

Semi looked at the young woman before her with half-shut lids. She had been broken, as they all are. The extreme shift from luxury to dungeon works every time. A couple of days down there and they either spill the beans or they die. Either way, it made no difference to Semi, except that beans could be served to her superiors. Dead informants told no tales.

"You were talking about Galium..." began Semi.

Jessamine remembered there was a young girl who stayed with them for a while. She was a timid thing, but she remembered Posie saying something about her having a barb.

Jessamine concocted an involved story of this girl, saying she was still in touch with Galium and they conspired together. The girl was growing now into a woman and rode around space on a vessel that well could be the Exterra they are looking for. She has a cohort with whom she exchanges information, one Arum, who is an ensign on a CG vessel under a Commander Belus. The two command a pirate vessel, one she was not sure it what it was called, but it was something about a snake or a squid.

Semi listened with wide eyes as the conspiracy unraveled before her. She heard the name, as close as Jessamine could remember it, that of Starburst, the mastermind and Arum, the junior officer aboard one of the top vessels of the Central Government. Arum managed the Commander from the side, where no one would expect the power to come from. His orders, straight from Starburst, steered the Commander and the ship according to his needs. In the wake of the destruction, the pirate vessel would sweep in and collect unguarded plunder, pillaging and raping at will.

The quiet and unsuspected mastermind behind the entire ring was young Starburst and her unlikely crew in their small and unassuming Exterra starship. And who was the one on top, who guided Starburst around the galaxy, avoiding Central Government troop vessels and outposts? It was Galium, of course, receiving information from Arum aboard the CG vessel and relaying it to Starburst aboard the Exterra.

Soon, she said, they would meet, do one last job, something about robbing a wealthy resort, and retire to a planet they had stolen where no one could get at them.

Semi sat back, exhausted from just hearing this wild tale of the most wanted conspirators in the universe. Galium, of course, was known and posted throughout.

The girl in the small retrofitted ship was suspected, but the description and names kept changing. Here at last was confirmation. And the added bonus of a mole, a source, a betrayer from inside a CG starship, this Ensign Arum, the right-hand-man of the Commander himself.

This was a game-changer. She could hardly wait to make the report to her seniors. And the one big final job had to be to plunder The Dark Side of the Moon itself, as no resort is as large or opulent. If they played it right, they could catch the turncoat, the pirate and the mastermind, all in one fell swoop. Yes, this was a revelation!

Damaged

"Number one-hundred and twenty-six has been damaged." said Flax. "There was not enough damage from the meteorite that struck it to send a distress call, and it did not explode. It did, however, send a request for maintenance, which got picked up by my automated request log. Being a repair vessel has its advantages."

"Well done, Flax. Is there a way you can respond so the request is listed as handled?"

"Already done, Captain. We should be there in time to catch the moon passing by. It will be a full moon for Earth, so it will be total darkness for the portion containing the resort."

"So, just to be clear, we can slip by without setting off the mines and it will be a short run to the lunar surface."

"That is correct, Captain."

"Are there any other vessels in the vicinity?"

"Three-hundred, forty-seven. Would you like a brief on each, crew, cargo and mission?"

"No, I forgot where we are, never mind."

Of all the shipping lanes in the Universe, those of Earth were the most traveled, especially in these days of increased empire-making. The CG was taking over every planet, every city, large and small. Each new addition to the empire began with a single vessel carrying the Grecian Flu virus, usually in a host, some unsuspecting person who will be the first casualty of the new epidemic. Then comes the medical ships, filled with doctors and vaccine, a daily dose of which will handle the flu. If you don't get your dose, you slip into a coma, never to wake. Those who fall in line behind the government goose-step get their daily dose of vaccine. Those who resist the CG takeover, don't.

The third wave is composed of ships filled with storm-troopers, those who will seek out rebels who have somehow avoided the flu and still oppose the government. After that, the Central Government vessels come and go as they please, taking whatever they want and leaving death and destruction behind them.

The storm-troopers are called "Peace-keepers." After they kill you, you are finally at peace. I wanted more than almost anything to correct that misnomer, but we had a task at hand already and I had to focus.

"Where is the best place to access the spa, Flax?"

"There are two systems in play, one on the upper floors, with camera and sound devices in every room, and one on the lower levels, under the ground. The equipment is also in every room there, but it is on a separate system. The upper level is the spa, which is luxurious. Music plays and the temperature is geared to the comfort of the guests. There are amenities to satisfy every desire. There are four meals served daily and snack-stops at every turn. Pools and sun rooms abound, cabanas such as the ones you described at the Wind Pools are in each section, complete with cabana boys to serve your every wish. Would you like your feet rubbed while you are there?"

"I doubt we'll have time, Flax, but I'll keep it in mind in case I see the boy from the Wind Pools. What is the situation with guards and arms?"

"There are no more than a handful of guards, armed with hand-stunners and trooper-sticks. If an alarm is tripped, steel gates close at every portal, allowing no one in or out. In that way, the guards inside will handle the intrusion. No additional forces can enter to aid them but no further pirates can get in either. Also no one can get out, so it can be a waiting game. They are not really sure what they are doing, as it is all guesswork. No one has attempted to intrude or escape. The resort has a flawless record."

"Hm. Yes. Sometimes a flawless record is just a matter of not reporting what you don't want known. Is there, I wonder, a way to plug into the resort system so that, if tripped, the doors can be opened again?"

"I will see what I can find out."

"Thank you, Flax."

"There is one thing, Captain."

"What is that, Flax?"

"There is a resort-wide alert that the guards on duty should be on the lookout for three vessels, including a pirate ship. The three are a CG vessel named the Ceberus, a Free Vessel Kraken, which is essentially a pirate ship, and an Exterra class named Bachinal. The pirate mastermind for this ring is called Starburst and is sent here by Galium. The CG reports have it wrong again."

"No, but that's par for the course with the Central Government. My guess would be that they have a few bits of information and are extrapolating from that, incorrectly, as usual."

"Well, if while on the ground, you run into someone named Starburst, I would be careful, they say she is armed and dangerous."

"Thank you, Flax," I chuckled. "I'll be careful."

The Serpent and the Dog

As we threaded our way through the most heavily trafficked space in the universe, two other vessels converged on the resort located on the moon's outward facing side. One was a pirate vessel named the Kraken, named for a giant serpent. The other was the CG vessel, Ceberus, the three-headed dog that guarded the gates of Hades in old Earth mythology.

Both vessels landed at Victoriana when we were there. The Kraken fired upon the trooper spheres advancing upon us at the Victoriana sky port. Captain Vikare's constabulary vessel fired upon the pirates, sending them to their heels. The Ceberus then attacked the Captain's ship, destroying it, resulting in the Captain taking refuge on board Exterra Bacchus.

"I would like to avoid meeting those two up close again, if possible, Flax. They are heavily armed and they do not hesitate to fire, ready or not."

"Agreed, Captain. We will dock with Palace Guard number one-hundred and twenty-six and prepare it for our entrance and future departure from the Earth's astro-space."

"Sounds good to me. Will you need me when you talk to One-twenty-six?"

"No, Captain. You should prepare for the landing on The Dark."

"Will do. Thank you, Flax."

"Aye aye, Captain."

I could not avoid letting a slight smile cross my lips as I rolled my eyes on the way back to the galley. Chineel caught my reaction.

"What has you amused?"

"Flax is talking like a pirate again."

"She enjoys the idea of it, thinks it's colorful. Let her have it."

"Oh, I will, but as you noticed, it amuses me."

"What has you amused, Captain?" asked Dione Ariadne, sitting at the table. She looked up from her warm morning ale, but I could tell she had been far away in her thoughts.

"Our ship thinks she's a pirate, that's all. She is

developing a colorful mode of speech that I find amusing."

"There's nothing amusing about pirates," Dione said, showing her serious side to be her only side.

"Yes there is," quipped Chineel. "I understand that on Earth before the Great Colonization, there were plays and stories about pirates that entertained and delighted the young people so much that they affected the ways of pirates, or at least as they envisioned them."

"Pirates are criminals and should be put to death without quarter," said Dione.

I leaned over the galley table with both hands to support me, putting my face into that of the young sergeant.

"You had better come to grips with the fact that in order to survive the next few weeks there are going to be things you'll do that you would never consider doing ordinarily. Like it or not, you are here with us and are one of us. There is no walking out in a fit of moral outrage. For good or ill, Sergeant, you are now a pirate. You had better get used to the idea."

"I'll never get used to the idea."

It was Chineel who put the young sergeant in her place. She put her face up to the sergeant's and whispered to her, nose to nose.

"Never is a long time, my sweetie. And space is a vast

expanse. You go with the flow out here or you go out the airlock, so if we all start talking like pirates, you'd better 'Arrggg!' with the best of them."

"Heave to, both of you, or you'll be keelhauled," I warned them. "There's two ships we've met before, one CG and the other FV."

"FV?" asked Ariadne.

"Free Vessel, unaffiliated, which in today's parlance means a pirate ship. Wait! Now that I think of it, we're unaffiliated. I suppose it means we are a pirate ship after all. I'll have to apologize to Flax and give her a 'shiver-me-timbers' or two." "What?" asked Ariadne.

"You're just going to have to keep up, little one. And understand, you may have been near the top of the food chain in the Icarus Constabulary, but you're on the bottom around here."

"Hey!" interjected Chineel. "Give the kid a break, she's as cast away as the rest of us. She just lost her shipmates, and her ship and her planet."

"Yes, of course. I am sorry for your shipmates. However, Icarus is still there, we can drop you off as we go by."

"No, we can't," scolded Chineel. "It's under the heel of the CG and she's dead, killed on Victoriana by, according to reports, the pirate ship, free vessel Exterra Bacchus. Or have you forgotten?"

"I haven't forgotten." I turned to Ariadne. "If events turn around in such a way that we return you to Icarus, you had better set the record straight as to who did the killing and who did the saving."

"You saved both our butts, the Captain's and my own. I won't forget."

I sat at the head of the galley table, fidgeting. I was agitated. We were risking all for friends we hadn't seen in years and complete strangers, and I was taking flack for the way I held my pinkie as we did. A good landing, goes the old saying, is one you walk away from. Looking good while doing it is an added plus, but not worth points.

"Settle down, sweetie," said Chineel, handing me a morning ale. "Fill us in on the plan, you like doing that."

I had to smile. Yes, I did like doing that. It made me feel important. After all I hadn't had a good chase through town and hadn't caused anyone's death in days, I had to do something.

"We're going to link with a defective mine, one of the many surrounding Earth and its circling moon. We'll set it to allow us an exit as well as an entrance and then slip down to the resort. Once inside, we'll find Jessamine and make our escape. I understand the CG presence is minimal at the resort; no one wants to break out."

"I could stand a week or two there," said Chineel. Dione frowned. She was still not used to Chineel's humor.

"Perhaps the CG hasn't taken over the Wind Pools. I could do with a visit there ... or we could just swing by and kidnap Ariel."

"Ah! That works! Then we'd have him all to ourselves."

Chineel and I laughed, with Ariadne in the middle, bewildered. Our laughter attracted the rest and soon Dagon and Runyon were at the bay door looking at us with curiosity while Ares and Aristaeus stood at the door to crew berthing with similar looks.

"We were just wondering if we could invade the Wind Pools and snatch Ariel."

"Ah!" said Aristaeus. "Foot rubs. Yes, that would be nice."

Ares looked at him. Aristaeus simply said, "I'll explain," and guided him back to the rear bay to continue diagnostics.

Dagon shook his head. He was having a hard time understanding humor, having never experienced it on his home world of Pallas, the planet constantly at war. He tried to explain us to Ares.

"They've been talking like pirates again. They do that from time to time. They think it's very funny. I don't quite get it, but I try to be understanding."

"I'll do my best as well," replied Ares.

Palace Guard #126

The starwort flower is supposed to be medicinal for an ache in the side. I wished I had some at the table, because I laughed until I had an ache in my side. But then, I have, in my time, caused more people to have a pain in their sides than to have made them laugh. I deserved a good laugh at this point.

As relaxed and funny as we had been in the galley, it was that tense on the bridge as we approached Mine Number One-twenty-six. As far as we could see to the left, again to the right, above and below, were mines, all lethal and all poised to blow if the net was disturbed. Only one-twenty-six was willing to receive us, the benign repair vessel that was there to fix it and make it right.

The docking procedure was simple and standard. The Exterra would drift at landing speed up to the pin, dock and extend a series of connections to be received by the mine on its underside. We would remain in this position, turning with the Earth, moving in its orbit, until the lunar orb caught up with us. We would then read in an instruction and pass through the net, releasing the connectors in the process.

It would then be a short trip down to the moon on the far side from the Earth to where the resort was set up under seven atmosphere domes. We had usurped the landing orders of an Exterra class shuttle.

My knuckles were white as we docked with the mine, though I didn't really do anything except watch. Everyone breathed a sigh of relief when the pin connected and the ship lurched, then stilled. We were docked.

The connectors went out and there were green lights across the connection panel. Flax was talking with Palace Guard #126.

In the next quadrant over, the Central Government vessel Ceberus under the command of Commander Belus requested entrance through the net of protective mines. After checking and double checking his credentials and confirming that he had permission to be in this sector of the universe at all, the mines in that section were turned off. Their lights went dim and turned green, allowing the vessel through the net in a narrow corridor just wide enough to admit the Commander's starship. As the last of the starship's hull cleared the nets, the lights on the mines went white and then red, indicating they were once again engaged. Entering when the lights were red would be the last mistake one would make.

In a quadrant on the other side of us, an exterior port opened on the bottom of a starship and a cannon was lowered, targeting a mine at random. The mine was hit and exploded. The six mines immediately connected to it also exploded.

At once, a report was sent of a detonation of seven mines. A repair crew was dispatched immediately from the mobile station. By the time the crew arrived, the free vessel Kraken was nowhere to be seen.

As the Ceberus turned and aimed itself at the moon, the Kraken also turned and headed for the same target. Both had the resort as their destination. In the middle of all of this, the tiny and unarmed free vessel Exterra Bacchus was setting down on the landing platform on the dark side of the moon under borrowed landing orders.

Flax was able to rummage up enough blasters and holsters that everyone stepped out of the starboard bay armed. She was in full figure and dressed in the battle-ready unitard, complete with blaster and blade, all holographic, of course. It was the very image of my own.

She was not mocking me, it was a tribute, an homage.

Captain Vikare and Sergeant Ariadne were in their uniforms and fully armed.

Dagon was impressive in a leather tunic. He wore a large blade at his back and two blasters, one on each side.

Chineel was unrecognizable in fighting gear, a plated jacket over plated pants and a helmet that covered her hair and most of her face. It was complete with heavy gloves, with a panel for her trigger finger, should she feel the need to use her blaster.

Aristaeus and Runyon were both armed, but stayed behind to guard the vessel. Flax reassured me no harm would come to them. We were ready.

"Sensors suggest that Jessamine can be found in the Sensory Relaxation room, straight ahead," said Flax through my earpiece.

"Got it. Moving in." I began moving toward the building.

The doors opened as I drew near, geared to do so automatically when a patron arrived. Inside were a series of doors off of the main room. Two dozen orderlies and service personnel jumped as we entered. A dozen guests dove for cover. Three guests threw up their hands and begged for mercy, though we didn't threaten them. One orderly was on his knees. A large dark spot appeared on his pants. He was shaking.

"Sensory Relaxation room," I shouted over the tumult of screaming people. The orderly pointed over his shoulder.

A door to the left flew open with a bang. Three CG troopers came through with blast rifles at the ready. Once they saw we outnumbered them, they dropped their rifles.

"Clearly, these are not crack troops. This assignment must be considered cushy among the ranks," said Vikare. He and Ariadne went to work cuffing the troopers together while I entered the Sensory Relaxation room.

There was a naked woman on the table, covered only at the buttocks with a thin towel, and a tiny Asian woman with both hands on the naked woman's back. The attendant lifted her hands in surprise and the woman looked up. It was Jessamine.

"Step back, please," I said to the attendant. She did so without protest, her hands politely behind her back.

"Jessamine, come with me," I said.

"Oh! Who are you?"

"It's Star, Jes, get dressed, we're leaving."

"Wha... Star, is that you?"

"Get your clothes, we have to go."

"Uh, I don't really have any clothes."

"Then get something, we have to go."

Jessamine threw a robe around her and followed me, barefoot, out into the main room.

"Demure as all hell," I said, making Jessamine smile.

Through a side door, seven storm troopers made a noisy entrance. They were better trained and fired immediately, spraying the room with blue flames. Two orderlies, all three handcuffed troopers and a guest were killed in the first volley.

Captain Vikare and Sergeant Ariadne returned fire, dropping five of the troopers. Dagon opened up killing two more.

Chineel stood by the door with a blaster in her hand, she was holding the door and searching for a target at the same time. I urged Jessamine through the door. A throng of guests and service personnel also made their escape through the door out onto the sky deck.

A crash at the far end of the central room proved to be a door being blown. It must have been locked. It wasn't locked anymore!

Through it came more star-troopers, but in different uniform, these were geared for a field battle. These were not house guards like we had just bested, these were seasoned troops, killers every one. They opened fire and received fire in return.

Ariadne was the one closest to the door when it blew, but instead of folding with the blast, she turned to the doors with the eyes of a hunter. She held a blast rifle in each hand, taken from fallen troopers. She opened fire and the first row of troopers was cut down. When her rifles ran dry, she drew her sidearm and continued firing, protecting our rear as we moved towards the automatic doors leading to the sky deck.

From the door that revealed the first of the troopers came more men and more fire, but not at us, it was aimed at the troopers. In the lead, I saw the pirate captain who sought to contain us on Victoriana. He was here and was fighting the troopers on our behalf. He looked at me and smiled, but it wasn't a smile that said he was glad to see me. It was a smile that said his quarry was in sight and at last he could catch her.

Shots came from the Sensory Relaxation room. I saw Chineel whirl and fall. It was the tiny Asian woman, the attendant who was so polite and submissive. She had a deadly side.

I turned my blaster on her and fired. Blue flame enveloped the room and she cried out, cut in half. I spun around, catching Chineel in my left arm and fired at the pirate captain with my right. Dagon dragged us out of the door and across the sky deck. He pushed me toward Flax and stood behind me with both guns blasting as I made my escape.

At the vessel, Ariadne pushed Jessamine into the bay,

followed by Vikare and Dagon. I emptied the register on my blaster at the advancing troopers and pirates. The roar of the thrusters drowned out Dagon's cry as he threw me a fresh blaster and came to stand beside me with his own. He fired and took hold of me at the same time. We moved together into the bay and continued firing as Flax lifted off toward the giant airlock at the top of the dome.

My blaster ran dry. I held it, trigger depressed, shaking.

"I've got you," said Dagon, his arm around me.

Escape from Earth

As Flax lifted Exterra from the deck, the scene we watched through the closing bay door was bedlam. Spa staff and guests were running for their lives, some of them only in robes, others had shed their robes and were running naked. It was not a pretty sight.

The shuttle deck at the main spa building held three craft. Besides ours, I recognized the Central Government vessel, the Ceberus that assailed us at Victoriana. The other was the Kraken. The picture painted roughly across the bow was that of a giant serpent. Somehow the Central Government vessel and the pirate ship had followed us all the way from Victoriana. The CG vessel had come to stop us while the pirate vessel came to lend a hand and participated in our escape. The reason for the help from the pirates was pretty clear, the capture of Exterra Bacchus and her captain as treasure.

Dagon and Runyon lifted me from the bay deck and helped me to the bridge, where I strapped into the pilot's seat and gathered myself for a status report.

"What's happening, Flax?"

There was no hologram, no matching outfit, just all-business Flax reporting.

"We are initiating diversion measures, Captain. The ship is disappearing before the eyes of whoever is watching. We have made a clean takeoff and will sail through the doors before they close on us. We should make it to Palace Guard #126 before anyone else gets in the air."

"Good. Do you need me up here?"

"I have it under control, Captain."

"Then I'm going back to check the crew."

Though I was regaining my composure, I was still shaky. Dagon was quick to lend a hand. Runyon was at my other side, holding my arm a bit too tightly.

"I'm fine, Runyon. Thank you."

"Yes, Captain." Runyon let me go and Dagon took full charge of me.

"Are you alright, Aristaeus?" I asked as I encountered

him in the bay looking after Ares and Dione. Both had been wounded in the fight.

"Yes, Captain. I'm without damage. The Captain and his sergeant took fire, but nothing serious, thankfully."

Vikare stood holding his side with one hand and his arm with the other. He had been grazed twice but like Aristaeus said, it was nothing serious. Ariadne knelt by the floor and I thought she might be seriously wounded, but there was merely a graze on her left leg. Still, she looked up at me with tears in her eyes.

On the bay floor next to Ariadne was Jessamine holding Chineel in her arms. Jessamine was crying and rocking Chineel like a child. Chineel didn't move.

"I'm sorry! I'm sorry!" cried Jessamine. "It was meant for me. She jumped in the way. I'm so sorry!"

Jessamine hung her head. Her tears fell on Chineel's face. Over Chineel's heart was a single wound, the entry point for the fatal shot. Somehow, the tiny attendant's bullet found its way through the armor plating protecting Chineel.

I fell to the deck next to Jessamine, wrapping my arms around her and Chineel together. Next to me, I felt Dagon, his arms cradling me.

Behind me, Runyon and Dione were sobbing, holding each other for support.

"Let us get her off of this cold floor," said Vikare, his

hand on my shoulder.

I nodded and stood up with Dagon's help. We picked up my friend and First Mate, carried her to her bunk in crew berthing and covered her with a sheet.

"We should find something pretty to bury her in," said Ariadne, but Dagon put up a hand.

"No! She died in battle. She is a soldier. She will be buried as she is, in her armor."

We stood in silence around her bunk, unsure of what to do next. We had done what we came to do. We had found Jessamine and helped her escape, but my friend was gone.

Stowaway

We sat at the galley table, gathering our thoughts and thinking of what to do next. Dagon collected the guns and walked with them to the arms locker. Leaving blasters lying around a starship was not a wise idea. Once done, Dagon stayed to work in the bay. His way of dealing was to stay busy.

"Whoa!" came a shout from the bay. We all leaped up and turned to the bay door. My hand went to my side where my gun had been, but it was not there.

In the doorway stood Dagon holding a girl by the arm. She was dressed in a dancer's costume of translucent silks, a pretty face and lots of dark hair. She was frightened out of her wits.

In an instant, Jessamine was up and going to her.

"Aysu! Her name is Aysu. She dances for the men.

They call her Sirina, but her name is Aysu. She helped me when I was in the dungeon. Are you hurt, sweetie?"

"No, but I knew my days were numbered there, so when I saw your ship, I made a decision."

"We've got to help her. She helped me," said Jessamine.

"On course, we'll help her. Welcome, Aysu. You're part of the crew now."

The words should have come from me, but it was Vikare who said them. I looked at him. He noticed my look and back-paddled quickly.

"That is, if the Captain and crew agree. I just meant, that is," he paused. "Over to you, Captain."

"Thank you Ares." I turned to the new addition. "So, you are called Aysu."

"Yes. It's Turkish for 'clear as moonlight on water.' Ay for the moon and Su for the water."

"It's a good name. Welcome Aysu. We'll find you something more appropriate to wear. I'm sure Chineel..." I stopped. That wouldn't work. "No, Chineel can't find you anything to wear. Perhaps there might though, something in Chineel's closets. Dione, will you help Aysu and Jessamine find some things to wear?"

"Right away, Captain."

"The battle's over, Dione. Call me Starwort."

"Yes, Captain." Dione stood unsure as to which way to

lean and not fall over. "Starwort," she said as she withdrew to the crew quarters. Aysu and Jessamine followed her as children follow a teacher, even a young one.

"Starwort," I replayed her speaking of it in my head. The name that drew ridicule as a kid in school, and more from Galium after I left, now felt like a medal on my chest, earned with blood and loss. Let the Central Government come and do their worst. They will meet Starwort and will suffer for it. Let the pirates assail me, they will die in the attempt. In future tales of bravery and daring, none will giggle at the name of Starwort. Even Galium, if he survives long enough, will say the name with hushed reverence.

Deep in my heart I was glad I cut the attendant in half with my blaster. It would not bring Chineel back, but neither would the attendant boast to her friends about the woman she killed. There would be no joy in the lunar resort tonight.

There would be no joy aboard the starship Exterra Bacchus, either, for we were preparing a funeral. It was called burial at sea from the sailing ships of Earth.

The vessel was too small for burial pods, with limited space a line had to be drawn somewhere. Therefore, the body would be wrapped and set adrift in the vastness of space. Whatever followed after that was out of our hands.

Searching Cecrops

Sector Agent Honor Toth sat at the large desk in the Icarus Constabulary office. It had been the desk of the Captain Ares Vikare, the head of the constabulary force of Icarus.

"Senior Sergeant Phaeton!" yelled the Sector Agent.

It had been the third time that morning he found it necessary to summon the sergeant twice.

"Coming sir," muttered Phaeton.

It insulting that he had to kowtow to this bounty hunter. Toth was not even an officer, not even a member of the Icarus force. Yet he asked for impossible things to be done in no time at all. Fetch this, find that, research something else. It was maddening!

"I want full reports from all field constables as soon as

they come in. Don't wait until the end of the day. If this man Galium is hiding in the city..."

"I know, sir, you want to know immediately and not after he has slipped away."

"Have I told you that before, Sergeant?"

"Yes sir, you have."

"Well, then, you should know it by now, shouldn't you!"

"Senior Sergeant," murmured Phaeton as he slithered out of the room to round up the precious reports.

Honor Toth smirked at the retreating sergeant. He knew his title was "Senior Sergeant," it was just that he had never known anyone to stress the point to the degree that Phaeton did.

Honor looked over the existing reports again. He had to be sure he was staying on top of all the information. The Central Government overseers could arrive at any moment to catch him not informed on some minor point.

He wished he had returned to base immediately after the wedding. He wished he had gone with Starwort on her insane mission. He wished... "And if wishes were fishes, beggars would feast," said Honor to himself, repeating the old childhood rhyme.

He hadn't gone back after the wedding and he hadn't gone with Starwort, he'd stay just long enough to receive orders relayed by the Central Government on Earth, orders to scour every corner of Icarus, indeed all of Cecrops, for the wanted criminal, Galium.

Honor knew where Galium was. Or at least he knew where Galium wasn't. He wasn't on Cecrops. He had watched the most wanted man in the universe lift off in a Cyrene 21X for parts unknown. But to report that would be to admit that he held the fugitive in his palm and had not closed his hand. It could be intimated that he knew the whereabouts of the man and was simply not saying. To do that was to commit treason and treason was punishable by death. Death was not a viable option to searching the city for a wanted man. So he searched the city for a wanted man. No paving stone would go unturned until he found the fugitive, or until he was reassigned by wiser men to a more reasonable task.

The great doors at the front of the hall banged open, making every constable in the place look up. Two Central Government Troopers walked into the main room and stood at the door, scanning the room for threats. Between the guardian troopers strode Commander Diphues, the CG Overseer, directly landed from Daedalus where he had just given the Daedalus Constabulary a well deserved shellacking.

There had been two dozen constables at the two dozen desks of the Icarus Constabulary when he first walked into the Headquarters. They were now down to nine, which was, in the Commander's opinion, more than were needed to do the job.

As fear froze the nine remaining constables where they stood, Commander Diphues marched back to the office of the Constabulary Captain, a post now held temporarily by a wild man of the lawless planets, a Sector Agent.

"Report, Agent!" said the Commander, in a voice louder than needed.

"Sectors one through seven are clear. There is no sign of the fugitive, Galium. I plan on visiting sector eight later today, several constables and myself. We believe he is being protected by local rebels."

"What is being done to seek them out and destroy them?"

"We have searches going 'round the clock."

"I count nine on the floor. Who is doing these searches?"

"They are, and I am. I used to have more men. Perhaps if they have not been executed, they could be returned to duty..."

"No, they cannot. They have been removed for a reason, Sector Agent. This is not Ceres, this is Cecrops. We have rules here and even Constables must abide by them. In fact, Constables should set the example. You are used to operating where there are no rules. We don't do that here."

"Yes sir, perhaps I would do better in a lawless land such as Ceres, where I can..."

"The Central Government has seen fit to saddle me with you and here you will stay until they remove you for completing or failing to complete your mission, which is the more likely."

The Overseer let his words sink in. He could hardly wait for Honor to fail at his mission.

"And the same Central Government has saddled me with you to dog my steps and question my every move. How, exactly is that helping?" asked Honor, through his teeth.

"Perhaps if I step up my visits to your office, pick up reports twice a day rather than daily. Would that be a proper incentive to produce results?"

The Sector Agent opened his mouth, but the Commander turned around and strode out into the common room, past the constables and out of the front entrance. The two troopers smirked, turned and followed him out, having proven once and for all that troopers are better than constables.

"Idiot!" said Honor, under his breath. The man was an idiot, but he was a powerful idiot and those are dangerous. The harder a man has to prove that he is of worth, the more likely it is that one could get killed crossing him.

"Sergeant Phaeton!" called out Honor Toth.

There was no response. Out in the common room, Senior Sergeant Phaeton stood at the main screen with his back to the office of his new superior officer. Every constable in the office had their eyes on him. He didn't move.

"Sergeant Phaeton!" came the second call. Phaeton didn't move.

"He's going to shoot you one of these days," whispered the constable closest to him.

"When he calls my name and proper rank, I'll answer. Until then, it must be someone else he is calling," replied Phaeton out of the side of his mouth.

"Sergeant Shem!" called Honor Toth.

Corporal Shem looked up from his desk, surprised. He was not a sergeant, he was a corporal, but he came running anyway. He stood panting at the Captain's desk, one hand pointing to his corporal's chevrons.

"Uh, sir, I'm not a sergeant, I'm..."

"You are now, Shem. Please give whatever you were working on to Constable Phaeton. Take this and file it in the orders of the day program. It's the updated list of non-commissioned officers. There are some changes noted."

Honor gave a data-wire to Shem.

Shem took the data-wire and nodded.

"Is there anything else, sir?"

"See that you arrive tomorrow with proper insignia, Sergeant. See that Constable Phaeton does as well."

"Yes, sir!" said the newly dubbed Sergeant Shem, backing out of the office.

Had he stayed, Shem would have heard Honor say, "I have to get out of here!"

Burial at Sea

We carried Chineel in full armor to the silver sphere Dagon had taken from the troopers on Khons. It was fitting. Chineel had come from Khons, where she had been married for a short time to my uncle.

"He was charming, once," she had said. "But then liquor would touch his lips and he became someone else. After a while the charming part failed to show up." She left him before I arrived, sent there by the authorities after the death of my aged parents.

No one ever asked how my uncle died and I never offered, even to Chineel. When there was no mention of a possible random visit, she refrained from asking questions.

Chineel became my First Mate. She respected me as Captain and we trusted each other. How many people can say that about anyone they know?

I attended the ceremony in battle dress. Flax echoed me, in her fully padded unitard as well. It was just a holographic likeness, but it was out of respect. As the sphere was brought into the airlock, I was able to get out a few words before choking up.

"Chineel was always one to serve the living rather than grieve the dead. I will honor her by doing the same."

That was all I could say. If more words were there, I didn't know what they were and couldn't get them out anyway. Others said things and I'm sure they were heartfelt and eloquent; I didn't hear them.

We stepped back into the bay and closed the inner doors. When the outer door was opened, Dagon fired the thrusters remotely and sent the sphere into the blackness. Chineel was with the stars.

In the galley, I sat at the far end, far from the Captain's chair. As I stared into emptiness, nothing registered but a cup of hot morning ale put before me. A thought darted through my mind that perhaps I should have an alcoholic drink, something strong to bolster my courage. But I had stopped drinking long ago and there was nothing of the sort on board. My next thought was that it was all for the best. If I started drinking intoxicating spirits it would not honor Chineel.

"Chineel stopped drinking the day she stepped onto the ship," I said, out of the blue. "I found her at the Mithra Tavern in Sterope on New Babylon. As the Wind Pools are fine and exclusive, Sterope is the opposite, a drunken, brawling port for pirates and poets. I never met any pirates that I know of, but lots of poets who fancied themselves pirates. I don't think we knew what that meant, we just wanted to be colorful."

A quick glance around the table told me all ears were on me; certainly all eyes. Even Flax, standing full-figure and free of the console, gave me her undivided attention.

"Chineel was there after I was; we didn't know the same people. My bunch was colorful; her bunch was not. You should have seen her: A gigantic green feather in her hair, dressed in a black and red iron maiden, pushing her up and over the top. All the men stared and glared. She held her guard up and wise-cracked with the best of them. I guess it was the sort of life that had an edge to it, but there was no future there."

I stopped, reflecting that there was no future for her here, either. I sucked in a mouthful of air and looked around. Jessamine and Aysu were both in tears and holding hands.

"I went with a mutual friend. He helped me talk her out of there. She came with me to help find my father's treasure. We found some, didn't we Flax?"

"Yes, Star, we did," said Flax. "You bought my contract and made me autonomous. No other vessel in the universe can boast autonomy."

"And we found my father's planet, Planet Bacchus. Galium says it has a green side, but all we found was dust."

"We should return to find the green side," said Flax.

"We will, Flax. Papa Posie has the key."

At that Jessamine looked up, suddenly aware and part of the conversation.

"Papa Posie? Yes, he said he had the key to Bacchus. I didn't know what he was talking about. The people who lived there before were named Bacchus, they died and Papa bought the house."

"Where is Papa Posie?" I asked, getting to the point.

"Shu. He has friends who live on Shu; it's on the outer rim. The Central Government won't go there. Too many of their troop vessels have disappeared in that quadrant. They tried to make it a prison colony, but couldn't get a foothold. The bunkers are still there, but I hear no one goes near them."

Abigail's voice came back to me, in my dream she said, "Silver globes attacked you but a silver globe will save you. The child in your care will care for you as an adult. The playground is a prison and a prison is your shoe."

It was exactly that, silver globes, CG Spheres attacked us, but Dagon saved us by stealing one. He left his precious speeder behind, but saved us with the sphere, a silver globe. Dagon cared for me, a child, though on the verge of becoming a man. The playground was the resort on the moon, but it was a prison, and the prison is in your shoe, only it's the planet of Shu which used to be a prison.

Shu was the furthest of the outer rim planets and there are wild things that live in the badlands. It didn't take well to colonization. There are a few political prisoners still there but it's mostly pioneers looking for a fresh start - and a refuge from the Central Government.

"There are also wild beasts in the outlands," I said. All heads turned toward me. Jessamine spoke up and the heads and eyes turned to her.

"Yes, I've heard that there are. Posey said he'd face wild beasts before he's face the Central Government."

"He'll face both before long. We'll need fuel before we get there. Where is the register, Flax?"

"Above half, but you are correct, we will have to stop at a refueling station. That will mean a new identity and a permit. The station we visited before is not returning a hail. I believe it has been taken out of service."

"Flax, can you check to see if the station was raided by pirates or terminated by the Central Government?"

"Checking, Captain."

No one spoke while Flax was silent. We held our breaths for the report. When she looked up, she had a note of sadness in her voice.

"The station was closed as a safety hazard. It has been destroyed. There is no record of the crew being redeployed."

The words came from my mouth without my bidding:

"Another way the Central Government is protecting us."

Earth

The Cyrene 21X interplanetary craft approached the docking platform north of Paris. The landing permit, passage documents and embedded identity chip proclaimed the arrival of Genus Nimrod, emissary of Kronos on the far edge of the middle ring. With the title of Ambassador, emissary Nimrod could expect to be admitted to the highest offices of the Central Government as well as the most exclusive social clubs.

The golden document he carried bore the official stamp of the High Commissioner of Kronos and was tied with the red velvet ribbon of the Senior Cardinal as well. It was the Ambassador's admission ticket to have audience with Seb, the Supreme Leader of the Central Government.

As the CG guard approached the vessel, Galium looked in the glass and adjusted his tie.

"No backing out now!" he said to the glass.

One final check in his full-length mirror said he was ready to meet the Supreme Leader of Earth. As ready as he was going to get, anyway.

"Demure as all hell!" said Galium. It was a favorite saying of an old friend, one he revered.

The Ambassador was scanned as soon as he stepped from his vessel. All was in order.

The Captain of the Guard frowned. He didn't like it when all was in order. It was a sign that something was amiss; it was too easy otherwise. He liked complexity.

The Sky Deck shuttle waited as Ambassador Nimrod's landing permit was checked and double-checked. His passage documents and implanted chip were scanned again, just to be sure. Galium suffered through this indignity with stoic visage. He had suffered worse for less-valuable rewards.

He would be admitted to the presence of Seb, the man who answers to no one, the place where, to quote an old saying, the buck stops. Galium didn't know what that meant, but it sounded good. He assumed that even a fully-pointed alpha-deer, the lead buck, would bow to such a person and therefore would stop at him. He didn't care if it was right or not, Seb was the man where the buck stopped and Seb was the man he came to see.

At the Grand Palace in the center of Paris, where the security was the highest on the planet, Ambassador Nimrod was scanned upon entering the outer doors, at the inner lobby, at the inner doors and in the great hallway to the inner sanctum. He was scanned again as he passed through the parted curtains at the entrance to the garden.

"Ambassador Nimrod," said a voice. It was electronically enhanced and seemed to come from everywhere, but Galium knew it was from the other side of the invisible wall that separated the place where he stood from the other three-quarters of the garden.

"Your excellency," replied Galium with a bow.

"Welcome to my garden." The figure of a boy on the verge of becoming a man stepped between two short bushes onto the stone walk. He wore a light tunic pulled at the waist and soft slippers. His hair was long and silver and seemed to dance in slow ripples behind his every graceful move. His smooth face showed not a trace or hint of a beard.

"It's very beautiful, Your Excellency."

"Oh, please, Ambassador, I am merely Seb, without grand titles. You may call me Seb."

"Thank you, Your... Thank you, Seb. I am Genus Nimrod, Gen to my friends."

"So, we are Seb and Gen, two simple men talking together. That is good."

The boy pulled a flower to him from the nearby trellis. He held his nose to the blossom. His eyes looked from the blossom to the man on the other side of the dividing glass.

"And yet you come with documents allowing you admittance to the most secure building in the known universe from some of the highest positions in the civilized planets. This leads me to ask:"

The boy let the flower go, showing an expression of appreciation, as if the flower had met with his approval and could therefore, it and all its offspring, continue smelling like that. He turned toward the Ambassador.

"What brings you to my garden, Gen?"

Galium smoothed his coat. In the process, he ran a fingertip over a dot on a card sewn into the lining. No alarms sounded. They were, for all intents and purposes, alone. Galium raised his head, activating another card in the collar of his jacket. The microdot on the back of his left hand began recording.

"The state of the union on Kronos, Your... I mean, Seb. Like many colonies, we have a desire to be more autonomous in our activities."

"What activities?" said the boy.

Galium knew that Seb was eighty-five years old. It had taken him most of that time to climb to this station in life, killing all of his opponents along the way. Seb enjoyed the cutting edge technology of the Center for Longevity and Youth. Six young men in their prime per Earth year were sacrificed so the supreme leader could enjoy eternal youth and everlasting beauty through their transplanted parts.

"The Central Medical Facility is not geared to many of the health issues found on Kronos. The surrounding planets have the same issue: a great deal of money goes to supporting doctors specializing in medical conditions not found locally while other maladies go unattended. As a result, there are doctors with nothing to do while hundreds die of maladies untreated."

"Yes. Go on." The boy touched a leaf, as if bored by the conversation so far.

"The Central Happiness Center is said to be caring for the general emotional health and well-being of the people, yet their only activity is the dispensing of medication, narcotics of every color and description. They deal, quite frankly in drugs. That is all. The portion of the population under their care grows daily, though they are not improving, but merely existing in a permanently drugged state."

"Has the Central Media been alerted to this problem?"

"The Central Media has been alerted. However, the Central Media only reports what has been sent to them from the Earth Central Media Office. It has yet to investigate any local issues. I'm afraid the Central Media, at least on Kronos, has no interest in the local situation."

Seb touched another leaf. A subtle smile crept across his face. The Ambassador continued.

"The Central Bank that funds these endeavors doesn't seem to notice what goes on, but provides an endless flow of money to them while ignoring local business and independent endeavors. When these things are brought before the local governors from the Central Government, the reports are received, but it's the last heard from them. In short, Your Excellency, Seb, we are at a loss. We would like to have a reason to go to work each day. The local Central Government doesn't seem interested in allowing us to do so. Instead, bribery and payoffs are the order of the day, special interests take precedence over real issues of the people and the members of the Central Congress are on permanent holiday."

Galium stopped, holding his breath. What he had just said was high treason. To criticize the Central Government, any of its arms or representatives, is against every law the CG cared to enforce. To do so to the highest official, the almighty Seb, was sheer lunacy. To criticize every branch of the government practically in one breath was suicide.

"I'm glad you brought this to me, so I can answer your questions and you can take the answer back to your people, and I hope this will lay the matters to rest."

Seb turned to Galium. His casual demeanor further softened. Below the calm, placid surface, Galium could sense sheer anger, so much so that if the unbreakable partition were not there, the Supreme Leader would have taken him and broken his neck. Instead, he looked down, composing himself, and then looked up, his large, blue eyes as calm as a lake in summer.

"The Central Medical Facility is dealing with the health issues of interest to the Central Government. The Happiness Center is following the edicts of the Central Government. They have the emotional and mental health of the planet under control, which is all we ask."

Seb turned his head and looked up at a leaf hanging from the closest branch. He drew in a chestful of air and continued at his calm, measured pace.

"The Central Media is reporting what it is told to report, which is what it should be reporting. The Central Bank is doing what it is supposed to be doing, funding these fine endeavors. And the officials of the Central Government are managing these organizations within given guidelines and to satisfaction. No reports of bribery, misuse or, as you say, an endless party, have come to me. In short, Ambassador, things are just the way we like them. If there is any disagreement, there can be a change made in the office of the planet's Ambassador, which should put an end to these fallacious reports."

Galium stood in the grand garden shocked by the Supreme Leader's words. He had no idea Seb would speak so candidly on the matter. What he said next was the most surprising.

"If that is all you have to ask, Mister Galium, would you be so kind as to leave my garden? I'm sure you have a transmission to send throughout the universe. I trust it will further solidify my position on these subjects."

"You don't seem to care about the people under your rule, Seb."

"You may return to calling me 'Your Excellency,' and you're wrong; I care a great deal, but the important words are 'under my rule.' They are indeed under my rule and you should remember that."

"The amount of graft, waste and misuse of power..."

"Oh, I don't care, Mister Galium. Do your worst. If an election were held today, no matter what candidates opposed me, even if you were running, I would win, hands down in an overwhelming landslide. The people are stupid. They are sheep, but make no mistake, they are my sheep. They do what I say and given a choice would not choose otherwise."

Galium took in a breath to respond, but there was an almost imperceptible click telling him the communicator to the other side of the glass had been turned off. Seb looked away, distracted by some other interesting plant or colorful flower. The interview was at an end.

Galium turned around, expecting armed guards to kill him, or at least take him prisoner. Instead, a powdered and perfumed hall assistant stood at the door in an elaborate suit and soft shoes. His hair was arranged in a high, outlandish wave, pale lavender to match his shirt.

"This way, Mister Galium. Your ship is waiting."

Galium followed the assistant through the same passages by which he had entered. When the great doors opened, he was taken by a single unarmed guard to his vessel. The guard saluted and turned around. As the guard left the landing platform, the doors on Galium's Cyrene closed. The thrusters started and the ship lifted off.

Galium went to the bridge to find the autopilot set for a little-known planet on the far end of the universe. The name of the preset destination was the planet Bacchus.

Serapis in the Distance

The weeks after Chineel's funeral were quiet. Flax kept us at cruising speed while she worked out the coordinates of our next stop and who we would be when we arrived. We would need another landing permit and another name, complete with identocard.

Aristaeus and Runyon worked on diagnostics and upgrades to Flax's systems. Aysu took over the galley and proved to be a fair cook. She was eager to be helpful. After all, she had stowed away aboard the ship.

My thoughts went back to the first day I leaped aboard the automated space repair vehicle. I was a stowaway. The take-off sent me to the floor, unconscious. I awoke expecting to be surrounded by an angry crew, ready to either put me to work or put me out the airlock. I hoped it would be the first. However, there was no one there. The life support systems were running because it would be expensive to turn them off and certain systems operated better in atmosphere.

Now here was another stowaway, only there was a crew to meet her. She willingly took up the chores of the galley. Without her hair done up and makeup, without the nails and eyelashes, she was a rather plain girl with large hands. She felt at home in the galley.

Chineel's closet did yield some items for Aysu and Jessamine to wear. There were alterations to be made, but a see-through dancers costume and a robe were not enough to go pirating around the universe. It seemed strange seeing a familiar blouse on someone else, but I knew Chineel would gladly offer it if she were around.

Dagon felt lost without his jumper or the sphere to work on. He had done all he could with the RRD, the Remote Repair Drone. He asked me several times what ports we were coming up on, in hopes that he could go ashore and steal another speeder. I had to tell him more than once that we took that speeder because men were after us, it was an emergency; we don't just go around stealing speeders.

In fact, I had done so more than once, but it was

always in a justified situation. Of course, Abigail used to say, "If it has to be justified, it's wrong. You're just trying to make it look right."

Dione and Ares tried their best to stay busy, but Flax had flown solo long before there was anyone onboard at all; she certainly didn't need help now.

I divided my time between familiarizing myself with the new innovations Aristaeus was installing and playing my clarinet. I bought the clarinet on one of my first ventures off the ship, in the same town where I met Aristaeus. I went to buy memory ewers and came back with the ewers, a clarinet and a story to tell. I came back with a friend as well. Aristaeus and I became close. I was glad.

As I sat on the bridge, playing folk tunes from my youth on Khons, a world came up on the screen: Serapis was in the distance.

"I remember Serapis, Flax. It was the first time I left the vessel for supplies after I came aboard. You gave me a Hermes for my pocket and I rode the RRD into town."

"Yes, I remember. You met a young girl with a tattoo around the scar where her implant was removed."

"Yes. She thought the scar I carry was from an implant as well."

"You did not contradict her."

"It's complicated."

Telling people my uncle cut me with a broken drinking

glass just before I killed him in self-defense could make for uncomfortable conversation. Abigail knew the truth. She kept my secret. Flax knew as well, and knew it was something better left in the past.

Flax was my friend and ally. She understood me. No living person did, though Galium tried. Abigail understood me, but she was no longer living. She didn't seem to mind.

My thoughts rolled back to Serapis, named for a deity of mythology as were most towns of the area. The girl was Acacia. The sisters in the dress shop were Day-Aysu and Nightshade, as different as their flowers and both of them mis-named.

"Lost in thought?" asked Ares, slipping into the co-pilot seat.

"Remembering my first visit to Serapis. We'll be stopping for supplies and fuel."

"Good memories?"

"Interesting, educational. In Serapis, I found a culture where the mandatory implanted chips of the inner ring were removed and one showed the scar with pride. Some tattooed around the scar to show it off. Others cut their clothing in such a way to show the scar, some had windows inserted in their clothing at the scar's location. A whole industry sprang up with the removal of implant chips."

"You can't move without them on Earth and all the inner ring planets. It's getting so you can't get far without them in most places on the middle ring as well."

"I bought a red blouse cut low at the neck to show off this." I leaned over and pulled my blouse aside, showing Ares my scar, the one I usually hid with clothing or my own hair.

"Is that from an implant?" he asked.

"No, it's from a childhood accident." Easier to explain with a little lie. I was a child and it was an accident that he didn't kill me.

"But people think..."

"Yes, and I don't correct them."

"Wise decision. When in Rome..."

"I remember that one, '...do as the Roman's.' It was many years before I learned what Rome and Romans were. Still, it made sense."

"So this is a land where no one has a chip," said Ares.

"Would it were so, Ares, but my friend, Galium - you remember Galium - he showed me something very interesting one night. He showed me a view of Serapis from above with everyone's chip glowing a different color. One was bright white. He said that person wouldn't be free much longer, the CG would come and collect him and his light would go out."

"How is that possible?"

"The CG made chips that could be programmed on the fly, so small you could hide them in tattoo ink. They injected the chips at the manufacturer, so the artist didn't know. A first chip would be removed and the person would get a banner tattooed over the scar with the word "Freedom!" or something like it. With the ink, another chip would be embedded. I don't know what the current state of affairs is on Serapis, but you can bet whoever goes ashore will have an identocard."

"An identodot," said Flax.

Ares jumped. He was still not used to Flax being omnipresent.

"How does that differ?" I asked.

"Just a dot on your arm, hardly noticeable yet with a full history in it, able to fool the most sophisticated CG scanners. Aristaeus has been working on it. The idea is not new, but the technology inside is smaller than the microchip in tattoo ink, barely a freckle."

I looked over at Ares with a mischievous smile. "I have interesting friends, don't I?"

"Yes, you do, Starwort, you do indeed."

The Augur

"So, Starwort," said Ares from the co-pilot's seat. "No man in your life?"

"I have Dagon," I replied.

"You know what I mean. I mean a special man."

"Oh, trust me, Dagon is special."

"Now you're playing with me."

Aysu slipped into the Navigator's seat behind Ares.

"Not at all, Ares, but you peer where your eyes do not belong. If I had interest, I would have said something. That I have not should settle all questions. If that changes, I will speak on the matter."

"So, no man in your life." Ares was being insistent.

"No," I said emphatically.

"Yes," said Aysu. We both looked at her.

Aysu went into a trance, her head rocked back and her eyes rolled to the side. She regained her control but closed her eyes, lost in a state.

"Three men are in your heart. Cupid fills your eye, though you have not seen him in too long. A man without a name in a crowded street still lingers on your mind. The third is one you recently left behind. You could not go with him and he could not come with you. All others are as leaves on the wind, flitting by without leaving a lasting impression."

Ares and I looked at each other. Aysu had talents we had not anticipated.

"What do you see before us?" I was careful not to use her name, as I had heard that in augury, one should not, for it could raise the person from the trance.

Aysu sucked in a mouthful of air. Her brows knitted, as if troubled by what she saw.

"The largest will fall, the smallest will lead and the lost will be found. The boy will be a man, the man will find a home and the orphan will have a family. That is all that I see."

Aysu's head hung forward, almost in her lap. Her hair hung down to her knees in an impossible tangle. For a moment she seemed as though she would fall off the seat, but then she caught herself and woke up.

"Oh, I've done something, haven't I?" It wasn't really a question. She knew what had happened. She'd done it before. It made people afraid of her.

"You went into a trance and said a few things. Nothing to be concerned about."

"Please don't hate me. I don't know what happens when I do that. I don't mean to hurt anyone. I'm not really dangerous."

"You have a gift," said Ares.

"More like a curse. I lose friends that way. Please let me stay with you. I like you. I think I could find a home here. You can use me. I'm good in the galley and ..."

Aysu was getting overexcited, as children sometimes do. I realized that regardless of her body-age, she was still a child.

"Shh! Take it easy, Aysu. Yes, you are good in the galley and we could use you. You're a welcome addition to our crew. Nobody's talking about casting you out. We haven't really discussed everyone's roles. People just do what they do. You picked right up in the galley and that's good. We'll just take care that you don't fall when you go into your trance, or whatever you call it."

"Thank you! I mean it, thank you so much! I don't know what I say when I'm like that. I don't even know if I'm right or not. People say I predict the future but no one's ever said I was right. No one said I was wrong either. Usually, after I do that, no one talks to me at all."

"Well, they're ignorant. We'll let you know if you're right. Every talent and ability is wild at first. You get used to your particular talent and you bring it under your control. It's like playing the clarinet. The first notes out of mine were horrible, but now I do OK - for an amateur."

Aysu smiled and sat back. She looked out of the side observation bubble for a minute and then said, "Something about a man, I think. Did I say something about a man?"

"Yes, Aysu," I said, heaving a long sigh. "...but not about anyone here. The man you mentioned is back in Icarus."

Ares took this in and nodded. He turned his attention to the passing darkness. Soon we were all looking at the stars and the space in between.

The Ceberus

Commander Belus looked over the lists of the wounded and the dead. He regretted the necessity of taking the soldiers from the resort aboard his vessel, but he needed men and could not return to home base to get them assigned. If he returned, they would need reports and updates, there would be the usual reassignments and the predictable, unnecessary changes. Minor officials would flex their muscles and show their power by coming up with obscure rules to be complied with before anything else could happen. Time would be wasted and the pirate vessels would escape him again.

No! Not again! He would take these pansies and make men of them. The dead would be off-loaded. The wounded would be left to recover at the resort and would catch up to him later or return to Earth for reassignment.

He knew, of course, that some would commit suicide before returning to Earth for reassignment. Others would find any transport they could, bound to anywhere in the universe. They would make their escape and tell tall tales about their wounds. More stories were told in the outer reaches about wild borth attacks than there were wild borths left in the universe. The giant canines were of some use as deterrents to escape in prisons, but the days of them running wild were a thing of the past. Still, to explain a scar or a limp, a wild borth story was as good as anything.

Belus sat in the pilot seat on the bridge of the Ceberus pondering his mission and waiting for the fuel to be loaded. He was not only stripping The Dark Side of the Moon of troopers, he was stripping it of fuel and food reserves as well. Several dancing girls and masseuses were also added to the crew list for the entertainment of the troops. There was a full wet bar in the lounge that was barely damaged in the firefight, but he declared it to be destroyed beyond saving. He ordered his troopers to load it into his ship: lock, stock and barrel; or in this case: bottles, glasses and coasters.

The Exterra had somehow fooled the barrier of mines

and had slipped through.

"Such a clever girl."

He had her on his screen. The pinpoint of light in the corner of the viewer was deep crimson from the emissions of the Red Stroke Drive when seen from this distance.

"Not that clever, demon urchin."

Amun scurried up to him with the report from the docking station. The fuel was completely loaded. The doors were closing and the fuel ports were being buttoned up.

"Thank you, Amun. Is everything aboard that we want from this embarrassment of a prison?"

"Yes, sir. We're ready to go."

"Then get to your station and tie in. This is going to get rough."

The final latch was released and the Ceberus used its thrusters against the sky deck to push itself up and out through the hatch at the top of the atmospheric globe encasing the main structure of the resort. Fuel handlers and technicians standing at their stations as the engines were started died screaming as the blast hit them. Belus never heard their screams, his leaving took priority over their pitiful lives.

"Now," he said to himself. "Find me that vessel."

The Ceberus cut thrusters and engaged the Red

Stroke Drive in the mains. Any crew not sitting and strapped in were thrown to the deck. They were at the barrier of mines in minutes.

Belus didn't feel like slowing.

"Hail the Guard. Request passage."

"I've been hailing. There is no response."

"Demand a response! This is a Central Government vessel on mission."

"Passage has been denied. There is suspicion of a traitor aboard, a spy who has been delivering vital information to rebels."

"Phorcys and Ceto! That's a load of borth-dung! Who is this master genius who has circumvented our defenses?"

"The report says the name is Amun. It came from one of the prisoners of The Dark during interrogation. Until it is resolved, they will not let us pass."

"Choose the center-most mine, target and fire."

"Sir?"

"You heard me. Amun doesn't have the brains of a trebium scuttle. The report is wrong. Shoot the mine and get us out of here."

"Yes, sir!" snapped the junior officer.

Two blasts from the vessel ran out in front to the near point on the network of mines, converging on a single mine directly in the ship's path. The mine exploded, triggering six mines around it.

The explosion took three minutes to dissipate. It was all the time the Ceberus needed. Belus flew through the hole in the network and out into free space.

"Estimate the trajectory of that vessel!"

"Yes, sir. I have it."

"Set our course to follow but not to overtake."

"Yes, sir," said the junior officer at the helm.

"Not yet, daughter-of-sixes!" thought Belus. "I will have you, in my own time."

The Snake

Pytho took several minutes to collect his wits and his men from the battle of the resort lobby. The luxurious decorations and appointments were bullet-riddled and smoldering from blaster-fire. Five of his men were dead. Sixteen were badly wounded and could not carry on without intense medical help. He would have to leave them behind. Five were only slightly wounded and could continue, or at least they would continue, rather than be captured by the Central Government. The remaining crew were not enough to man The Kraken.

"Collect any remaining troopers and resort personnel. Gather them together in the lobby."

"The lobby is in shambles and might catch fire at any minute, Captain."

Pytho leaned in to put his mouth next to the ear of the man who spoke. He yelled his order.

"Then you had better assemble them quickly!"

The crewman ran off to do just that before he became one of the wounded to be left behind.

"Offer them a choice," Pytho said to his first mate, Agni. "They can join us, or they can remain here to answer to the Central Government as to why they let a prisoner escape leaving behind so many casualties."

"Aye, Captain. There'll be no holdouts, I'm sure."

The first mate trotted away chuckling. He loved giving the ultimatum to innocents left behind after a battle. They cringed so pitifully, cried so convincingly and in the end, became pirates, beginning at the bottom of the vessel's ladder: swabbies. Swabbies were always fun to torment.

"Captain, the government vessel is approaching the network at flank speed. I don't think it's going to open for him and he doesn't show signs of stopping."

"He's going to blow it!" shouted Pytho. "Everyone left in the resort, herd them into the bay. Get our crew aboard, everyone, everyone aboard. We're leaving!"

"What about those who don't want to join us?" asked the first mate, conflicted with the opposing orders.

"They'll go out the airlock, they can swim back to Earth. Snap to it, start thrusters, batten down the hatches and secure the guns. We're going to follow that ship through the net."

Crewmen flew in every direction, readying the ship for takeoff. Resort personnel ran aboard the pirate vessel rather than be left behind to face the Central Government cleanup crew. After such an outcome, anyone still alive was considered a conspirator and jailed without trial. Some were executed, others disappeared without a trace. Many were believed to still be in prison, though after a while in prison, death was a certainty.

It was said that nothing on Earth gave tribute to the dark ages of history better than the prison system. Disease ran rampant through its lower levels. Some prisoners died of starvation rather than eat the rations they were given. Others became killers with the agreement that after so many kills, they themselves would be killed and so released from continued incarceration. In the face of what was known and what was rumored about Earth's penal colonies, joining a pirate band was an easy decision.

Within minutes, the Free Vessel Kraken lifted off of the sky deck leaving no one behind. The few poor souls who hid in the basement or the far offices of the resort thinking themselves safe from the intruders, the pirates and the soldiers, would be left behind to face the Central Government Investigators.

The government vessel Ceberus blasted through the network of mines. The hole would take time to repair once it was reported and a repair vessel dispatched. Pytho saw an opportunity to pass through the net without making his own hole. The net would be harder to blast through a second time, but the CG vessel had cannons larger than his own. The Ceberus had no trouble with the net of mines known as The Palace Guards.

"No," thought Pytho. "The trouble would come later when it was reported that a CG vessel caused that kind of damage after fleeing a battle at the pet resort of the Earth senior corporate chairmen. No colony will be a haven for the Commander."

Agni approached Pytho, meek and apologetic. He had a question. It seemed important to him, but would it be to his Captain? Or would the Captain say he was stupid and kick him as he often did?

"Uh, Sir, that vessel, the Central Government vessel that just blasted through the net. Uh, why did it do that, sir?"

"Eh? What, Agni?"

"Why did it blast through the net? Why not get clearance?"

"Hm. You're right. All he needed to do was to get clearance like he did when he entered. Why blast through?"

The question was still on his mind as the Kraken flew at full speed through the hole in Earth's defenses left by the fleeing CG vessel.

Interceptor jets and ground-to-space rockets had been dispatched, but the pirate vessel flew at full speed. A small adjustment for trajectory and they were following the CG vessel into space.

"Now, where are you going, Commander?" asked Captain Pytho.

The Minotaur

Admiral Phanesh, Commander of the Master Fleet of Earth stood on the bridge of his flagship, the Minotaur, mightiest of Earth's war vessels. He watched the screen intently as seven junior officers poured over their own screens, each with two assistants. The objects of his interest were three in number.

The small dot in the corner of his screen, tinted green by his first mate, his right-hand man, Technical Ensign Eanush, was an Exterra class repair ship. The Exterra wouldn't ordinarily be of interest, except this one had been retrofitted to be automatic, removing the need of a crew, and yet it had been retrofitted again with some advanced technologies and once again boasted a crew. It was curious.

The second vessel to catch his eye is the Free Vessel

Kraken, which escaped his gaze while operating in the outer reaches but was now operating in his backyard. It had recently visited the Lunar Resort, The Dark Side of the Moon. What was a pirate vessel doing so close to Earth? The gall of the man! He must be squished like a bug, as an example if for no other reason.

"It's all right and well to go tramping about in the outer ring," the Admiral often said to friends at his club. "But to come within the inner ring, to come anywhere near Earth, borders on blasphemy. The inner planets are sacrosanct, out of bounds to them. It just isn't done, that's all!"

The third, and most irksome of the blips on his personal radar is none other than the Ceberus, a ship of the line, captained by one of his own students, Commander Belus.

"Belus!" The Admiral rolled the name around on his tongue. "Arrogant, rude, aloof, smug, always under foot and always in trouble. Wealthy father, of course, who got him out of everything. Sets a bad example, that."

"Sir?" asked T.E. Eanush.

"Broke every rule, Eanush. Cared about none of it. How he ever became a Commander is beyond me. The man isn't fit to captain a scow."

"Yes, sir." T.E. Eanush knew better than to get in the middle of a rant by the Admiral.

"Extrapolate those three trajectories, Eanush. Where are they going?"

"Right away, sir!" Eanush jumped to it, letting his fingers dance over the colored dots on his wrap-around screen. He had to reach for a few, his screen was so large. He had the biggest one on the vessel, the biggest in the fleet, and he was proud of it. Screen size was the subject of much conversation in the relax rooms and food courts of the Main Fleet. Eanush's, everyone knew, was bigger than anyone's. The men were envious and the women squealed just to speak of it. Now he was ready to report. Eanush stood at his station and turned toward the Admiral.

"The Free Vessel Kraken is tracking the Central Government ship, sir, neither gaining nor losing distance and on the same coordinates. It seems to be following the Ceberus. The Ceberus is itself stalking the smaller vessel. Commander Belus isn't chasing it down, nor is he lagging far behind. I believe he is trying to see where the smaller vessel is leading."

"And where is he leading, Eanush?"

"At this distance, it's difficult to say for sure. They could veer off onto another course between here and there, but the Exterra appears bound for Serapis. "

"Then that is where we will also go. Prepare a flight plan, we're going to Serapis."

A Storm Coming

It is so rare that I visit a place twice that the very idea of something being familiar is strange and new. The approach to Serapis was familiar, as was the landing area, far from town. A vehicle is needed to get there. The RRD would do it for us.

If the RRD had senscient recall, it would also remember the drive to town. The repair was a communication tower on the planet's satellite. I had nothing at all to do with it, I was the stowaway, a waif loosed in the world, a space bum.

At the time, I gathered spare parts and odd bits, bundled them up and traded them for food, there being none aboard the automated vehicle that was my home. I remembered Serapis fondly.

By the time we reached the planet, I had come to grips with Chineel's death and had made both Aysu and Jessamine into friends. With Aristaeus, Runyon, Ares, Dione, Dagon and myself, we had eight aboard, almost a full complement. Mealtime was a project and all pitched in. I wasn't used to so many people aboard. Everywhere I turned around, someone was there. Six bunks in basic crew berthing were occupied, near capacity.

I maintained the Captain's berth as I had since Chineel first suggested it. There were many things first suggested, first performed or first initiated by Chineel. She was gone, but still lived in every room of the vessel.

Aristaeus took the other solitary quarter, the mate's berth.

Flax, who was always omnipresent, now took to walking around the ship. Aristaeus soon got used to her looking over his shoulder as he worked, but Dagon never would.

Aristaeus had something on his mind as we drew near to Serapis. I could always tell with him.

"Yes, Star, my darling, you don't have to ask, there is something troubling me. Shall I spill, or are you keen to guess?"

"Don't make me guess, we'll be here all day," I replied, settling into the pilot's seat on the bridge.

"Serapis is where I sent my household staff and several of my friends and their families. I will have to see how they are doing and if they're thriving."

"Naturally. Now my question is, to what degree is the answer going to affect the next leg of our journey."

"You unmask me. Yes, the answer to the question, 'How are you doing?' will shape my decision to stay or to leave. This, that is to say, you and Flax, are the closest I have to family. Dagon and Chineel as well. Her loss touched me deeply, but it has no bearing on the decision to come."

"What will shape your decision?"

"I've given that a lot of thought and even discussed it with Flax, during our late-night talks here on the bridge."

"I knew you two were hatching something."

"Yes, and here it is. Serapis is, or has been reported to me to be, less under the thumb of the Central Government than many of its sister cities. If all is well, everyone is thriving and it is a good place to set up, I may want to stay. Runyon was interested in one of my neighbor's serving maids and I could build a shop and continue working on several of my pet projects. If they are doing well and are living free, I may make my goodbye's at Serapis."

"If that's the case, I will miss you, but I will understand."

"I know you will. However, if the CG has gained a foothold, if every lock opens with an implanted chip, if armed guards on the streets are commonplace, expect me to fly on to the next port of call. I might even bring a few people with me."

"They should bring bedding, as the crew berthing will be full."

"I'll see to it. The challenge will be if Serapis is completely unlivable and I have to bring the entire lot with us to Shu, or even to Planet Bacchus. If they have made a home on Serapis, so be it. But if I have sent them to a place as dangerous as Victoriana or worse, they might have to come with us."

"How many are we talking about?"

"Well, mind you, it may be possible to simply put them aboard the vessel that brought them from Victoriana and to just meet them at Shu. We'll evaluate the situation there."

"You're avoiding the question."

"Thirty, possibly forty. It would be difficult to fit them all in, I know, but if the vessel isn't functional, if they must move on to be free..."

"Say no more, Aristaeus. We will evaluate the situation and make the right decision. If we leave Serapis with forty or fifty more people, we'll sleep in shifts and make it work."

"And if Shu proves to be unworkable?" Aristaeus looked at me for the first time since I brought up the subject. I had to make a decision now that I would stand by later.

"Than we'll eat and sleep in shifts all the way to Bacchus and establish a colony there."

"Thank you, Star. You warm my heart."

Aristaeus leaned over and hugged me. It was awkward in the bridge seats, as the co-pilot was not in the habit of hugging the pilot, so the seats were not designed for it, but Aristaeus made it work.

"I can assume," I said, knowing that Flax was hearing every word, "you are in agreement?"

Flax's holographic head materialized above the bridge console. "Of course. There may be some changes in the facilities if there are that many in the party, but function always monitors structure, not the other way around."

"Wise Flax," said Aristaeus. "Thank you, my friend. You always have my back as I have yours."

It was a strange feeling, but secretly, I was hoping we would have to face the challenge of taking thirty or forty people with us to Bacchus to start a colony.

"There's something my father said that just occurred to me," I said to both Aristaeus and Flax. "If your vision doesn't frighten you and invite ridicule from others, it's too small."

"Oh! Well!" said Aristaeus. "Then let us consider enormous visions only."

"We are landing at Serapis, if anyone is interested," said Flax.

"Anything on the sensors that makes your skin to prickle?"

"Nothing so far, Captain, but dress for harsh weather, there's a storm coming."

A Chilly Welcome

Serapis, named for a Greek-Egyptian god of the 3rd century BC, had nothing to do with the Greeks or Egyptians. The ancient people and places of Earth's history - and often mythology - were used to give names to the towns and planets of the colonies. Those who came from Earth were fond of keeping such things alive, even if the inhabitants of Earth were not.

The metal plate of the free-dock was familiar. Flax revved up the RRD and set it to auto-pilot for the center of town. I climbed into the back seat with Dagon. Aristaeus climbed into the front with Runyon. It was, after all, their mission more than ours.

Flax plugged into the refueling station while Aysu and Jessamine looked to the chandler's for food to stock our pantry. The Chandler was pleased to bring a floating extension of his store to the vessel for the ship's galley staff to purchase.

Ares Vikare and Dione Ariadne stood watch over Flax and the galley staff. Ares had an itch he could not scratch and Dione had worked with him long enough to respect his instincts.

Flax made identodots for all of us, those who left the vessel and went into town, and those who stayed on the ship alike. From what I knew, the CG looked at this place from afar. The only question to be answered was whether the locals knew it or not.

As it was the Captain who was going ashore, I dressed the part in my armored unitard, complete with blaster. I turned to the full-length mirror and pulled my hair over the scar on my neck.

"Demure as all hell," I said to the mirror.

The outbuildings at the edge of the free-dock, once abandoned and empty, were now repaired and manned by port agents. As we went through the sensors, four blips sounded, reading the four identodots. We must have been cleared because we were allowed through without incident or question.

The RRD ran to the center of town and stopped at the

fountain, where it had dumped me out on my last visit. I took the lead and went to the cafe, as that was known to me.

The girl who waited on me before was not there. In her place was another girl, taller with dark hair. Her scar was readily visible over her low neckline. Around her scar was a tattoo of a heart with the inscription, "Follow your heart."

"Morning ale?" she asked.

"Yes, please, four," Aristaeus said. We found a table and sat down to enjoy morning ale and watch the day as it turned dark with the coming storm. No one else was at the cafe and no one else came while we were there.

"Where is everyone?" I asked.

"Were you expecting someone?"

"No, it's just that I would think there would be customers here and people passing by. Is the storm keeping them in?"

"No one ventures out. To do so brings attention."

"I knew a girl who worked here, Acacia. Is she still here?"

"No one is here by that name." The girl turned and disappeared into the back of the cafe before I could ask more questions.

"The girl who was here before bid me travel well and said she would remember me. It is a common saying in the outer lands, as it is unlikely you'll ever see the person again. I suppose it was more prophetic than I thought."

We finished our morning ale and pressed a Ц20 into the girl's hand. She looked at us with suspicious eyes and turned to go, not even offering change. I was going to suggest she keep whatever was left over, but the option was not presented. When I had visited before, the people were friendly and open. Now the opposite was true.

"The shops are this way," I said, pointing up the street.

On the narrow street I had walked once before, much was changed. There were no colorful flowers in the window boxes, no smiling people at the doorways and windows. There was no one visible at all.

At the first shop, a store for general goods, stocking just about everything but not very much of anything, the door was closed, but there was light inside. I tried the door and it opened at my touch. Inside was a woman of advanced years with a stern look on her face.

"Hello, and a good day to you, madam," began Aristaeus. "I am looking for friends who came here just recently."

The woman's expression changed to surprise. "Genus?" she said.

"Yes, I am Doctor Genus. My people are here? Do you know where they are?"

"Yes. They are with the Protectors, the Peacekeepers. They came without implants. The Protectors didn't know what to do with them, so they are being held."

It didn't make sense to me, so I pushed by Aristaeus and inserted myself.

"But many here, I understand do not have implants, they have been removed. An artist by the name of Hermes often tattoos around the scars. We have seen his work on the girl at the cafe."

"Yes. Hermes is here and still makes his art. There are those with implants and those who have had them removed. Hermes draws around the scar. For some reason, the Protectors leave you alone. Perhaps they are lovers of body art."

"Yes, of course. Thank you. Where are the recent arrivals being held?"

"At the Peacekeepers, of course. You are new here, are you not?"

"Yes, we are, we've just arrived and are here to visit friends." I replied, trying to sound as innocent as possible.

The woman darkened. She didn't like the idea of new people.

"Center of town, biggest building there. You'll see it."

Yes, we did see it. It was built up to three stories, while the rest of the town was all one level. Armed guards surrounded a structure that took up an entire block between streets.

"What's with the tattooed people again?" asked Runyon.

"Those who have had their chips removed are in violation of the law here, but you can't arrest everyone, so the CG put tracking ID implants in the tattoo ink using micro-nano technology. The implants are so small that they are undetectable."

"This is the first time we've encountered that particular technology," said Aristaeus.

"Galium says it is still having the bugs worked out. When there are two implants, the more recent flushes the older one out, but sometimes it goes wrong and the person dies. Death is an unpopular outcome."

"So, they are still working out the kinks."

"Yes. I'm going to contact Flax and then we can go in."

"I'm listening in, Star," said Flax in my listening dot on the back of my ear.

"Good. Then you know we're about to walk into the lion's den."

"There are no transmissions coming from that building. It might be a dead zone."

"We'll be careful. Let's go, gentlemen."

Peacekeepers

Aristaeus inquired at the front desk and we were taken to a conference room with many chairs around a large, oval table. We waited until a senior official entered. When he did, he was wearing a sash of office and looked as if we had interrupted his break for morning ale.

"What is it? I'm a busy man!"

"A vessel from Victoriana brought passengers recently," began Aristaeus. "They are known to me and I wanted to extend my greetings to them. I understand they are held here?"

"Held until an official representative of the Central Government can arrive to determine their fate. They came without chips. Without chips, how can we know who they are. We have a hard enough time with the locals, all those tattooed scars. How Central puts up with it, I'll never understand. When the representatives arrive, we'll find out."

"May we see them?"

"You may not."

"May I speak with one of them?"

"You may not."

"What may I do with regard to them?"

"You may leave. I'll remember you." The Peacekeeper senior officer left without further word.

"Time to go," said Flax in my ear.

I tugged on Aristaeus's sleeve. Dagon had also heard Flax's order and was already guiding Runyon out of the conference room.

On the street, not a word was spoken. We returned quickly to the RRD and urged it back to Flax with more speed than upon our arrival. On the way, we passed the Candler's hovercraft making its way back to town.

At the bay door, Ares and Dione were standing by with full uniform and side arms. Ares pulled me aside.

"If I may, Captain, let me have Dagon and Runyon in fighting gear. They will be our official guards."

"Do you have a plan?"

"If we can find a transport."

"Flax," I spoke to the air. "Call back the Chandler's

craft."

Within minutes, we had purchased everything aboard the chandler's hovercraft and had rented the vehicle for the rest of the day. The chandler was not a fan of the Peacekeepers and went along without protest. He was coming out alright at any rate.

Flax affixed new identodots to the four of them, identifying them as Central Government guards. We watched them sail off in the chandler's hovercraft.

We served the chandler and his daughter tea in the galley and chatted about Serapis.

"When did the Peacekeepers arrive?" I asked. Aristaeus puttered around the galley, trying not to look interested, while Aysu and Jessamine did their best to act like lowly kitchen maids. All our ears, including those of Flax, who was keeping out of sight, were perked for news of the new Serapis order.

"They came in the cold season. A vessel landed and the Peacekeepers stepped out. They were armed and had orders removing local governors and replacing them with their officers. They replaced the constables with their troopers. A few protested, but were never seen again. They began implanting the people with those identity chips. Not everyone, just those who had not had them. Some removed their chips, but the Peacekeepers didn't do anything about them. Hermes gives those who had their chips removed a tattoo to celebrate their freedom. It seems to work, for the Peacekeepers leave them alone."

"They are getting a newer, smaller chip. It's in the ink Hermes uses. It's not his fault, he doesn't know."

The chandler looked down at his forearm, at the inch-long scar and the flourishing banner proclaiming "Freedom!" in bright blue.

"Chips in the ink?" he said, his voice breaking.

"Yes, so small, even the artist doesn't know it's there."

"Incredible to believe!"

"Sorry," I said, as if it would help. The chandler's daughter pulled her blouse forward and glanced down to where I assumed she also had a scar and a tattoo.

She looked betrayed. They both did.

At the Peacekeepers' headquarters, Captain Vikare walked in like he owned the place. He presented a reader with documents provided by Flax as his armed staff stood by. The desk sergeant thought the two guards looked familiar but could not remember from where.

Twelve ragged prisoners were escorted to the front desk.

"There were thirty," said Captain Vikare.

"Some protested," said the desk sergeant in reply. It was the only answer they would get.

"There was luggage," said Vikare.

"Confiscated!" said the desk sergeant, glaring at the

Captain.

"This will appear in my report." Vikare glared back at the desk sergeant, the only Peacekeeper present at the exchange.

"Then you'd best get to it," said the desk sergeant through his teeth.

Captain Vikare waved his hand and his three guards guided the weary prisoners out to the waiting craft.

"We're on our way back," reported Vikare. "We have twelve, but we're not even sure if they are the right twelve."

"Hello, Runyon," said one old man, coming more alive with the cold, fresh air of the outside.

"Hello, Mister Balder. Are there any still in there?"

"No, Runyon, we are all that are left after the Peacekeepers quelled our protests."

"I see your wife and our maid and... who's the fellow in the back there, in the faded red shirt?"

"Him? I don't know him. He came into the cell only minutes before you arrived."

Captain Vikare didn't even slow the hovercraft, he leaned back and lifted the stranger up, out over the side of the craft and let him go. The man tumbled into the dirt, surprised by the suddenness and ferocity of Vikare's attack.

"There you are, Runyon. You know the rest of them, is

that right?"

Runyon looked over the remaining eleven and named each of them. There were two staff from Doctor Genus's household and seven neighbors and two constables from the Victoriana Constabulary Force. In the eyes of the Central Government Peacekeepers, they were all criminals and equally guilty.

Sergeant Ariadne looked into the rear screen to see that another, similar hovervan had turned a corner and was following them. The hovervan didn't seem to be trying to catch up, but wasn't turning or falling behind either. It was clearly a chandler craft, as it was loaded down with food and ship's items.

"We are being followed, sir," reported Sergeant Ariadne.

Vikare looked back. A woman was driving the hovercraft. Both were traveling slowly due to the weight each carried. Vikare turned back around in his seat.

"She doesn't look threatening. Let's not raise our hackles just yet."

The hovercraft sailed over the metal sky deck toward the waiting Exterra. To his surprise, the port bay opened to admit the entire vehicle. As he pulled in, the second hovercraft pulled in as well. The bay door closed and Flax started the thrusters.

"Let's get everyone into the galley and sorted out," said

Flax, in a representation of my summer skirt and blouse, looking as non-threatening as possible. "Secure those vehicles, we're about to take off."

With all of us lending a hand, the hovercraft were tied down and their contents unloaded and put into hatches. We were still securing items as Flax lifted off. As soon as I could free myself of the all-hands stores-party, I got to the bridge and put myself into the pilot's seat.

"What's the situation, Flax?" I asked.

As we rose higher over Serapis, I could see two fully loaded Peacekeeper vehicles bouncing onto the sky deck. They had come over the unpaved lands on the way from town at such a pace that they raised a cloud of dust as high as Flax was as we continued to lift.

"The Peacekeepers have reconsidered letting you go with their captives, Captain."

"Isn't that a shame. Shall we go back, return them and apologize?"

"No, Captain, I don't think we will," said Flax. She had a giggle in her voice.

"And the Chandler?"

"It did not take him long to consider his options. He asked if he could come along. He called his wife to load the other craft and bring it. We have fourteen new hands aboard. Your prediction about sleeping in shifts is about to come true."

Hot Welcome

It became a matter of public record that the Central Government Ship-of-the-Line Ceberus landed at Serapis the day after our own departure. Commander Belus stepped from the vessel to meet the full contingency of Serapis Peacekeepers.

The Serapis Peacekeepers would not again be fooled by a false authority. When Commander Belus failed to produce traveling documents from the CG or a landing permit, the commanding officer of the Peacekeepers ordered the vessel impounded and the crew jailed. Commander Belus in turn ordered the guns of the Ceberus aimed at the Peacekeepers and all batteries to fire at will. In less than the time it takes to tell, the Serapis Peacekeeping contingency was leveled. Not a man survived.

Ensign Amun was dispatched to town to inquire as to recent vessels coming and going. He was told that the Chandler and his wife were missing. Also with them was their daughter and the total inventory of fresh vegetables. An alert was put out across Serapis to be on the lookout for the Chandler, his family and the vegetables. A description of his hovercraft was included in the report.

Having done all they could, Commander Belus and his crew engaged thrusters and took off, leaving the inhabitants of Serapis to bury the Peacekeepers and properly dispose of their weapons. A local civic leader named Hermes took charge of the burial and cleanup of the sky deck. The weapons were evenly distributed over the Serapis population in case a hostile vessel should ever again land on the sky deck.

A week later, the Central Government Flagship Minotaur under command of Admiral Phanesh sought to land at Serapis. The vessel was denied access, as the authorities there had never heard of an Admiral Phanesh, did not believe that a flagship of the fleet would ever come to Serapis and did not know what a Minotaur was. The Admiral's ship flew off following the signal of a CG ship-of-the-line since declared to be a "rogue vessel."

Waiting

Serapis returned to its former ways, removing each chip discovered within the population. The tradition of tattooing around the scar continued, though the artist Hermes began a search for another source of tattoo ink.

Exterra Bacchus, a vessel originally designed for nine, now carried twenty-two. The two Victoriana Constables were pressed into service as crew under Captain Vikare. The Chandler and his wife and daughter joined the galley detail to help Aysu and Jessamine feed twenty-two mouths. Two maids from Victoriana also joined the galley crew. The remaining new passengers made places for themselves in the bay and did their best to not get underfoot. Thus apportioned, we set sail for Shu on the outer rim.

When men talk of wild things, animals you cannot describe for lack of reference, they speak of Shu. The short lived penal colony turned to a settlement, then a town and now spread across a third of the planet, with schools, shops and houses of religious worship. There was a police force of a sort and a fire brigade, all volunteer. In the wild lands, beyond the frontier, things lived that could not be caught, were too quick to trap and therefore were never eaten.

We knew one person there: Papa Posie. If he wasn't at the sky deck when we landed, we were not assured of a warm welcome.

Flax searched the darkness for a beam from Shu to announce our coming. She found none. Meanwhile, the rest of us, as I predicted, ate and slept in shifts. I gave up the Captain's berth to the Chandler and his family and the Balder family alternately. The Balders lived next door to Aristaeus on Victoriana.

The added people filled crew berthing and the galley table in shifts. There was little room in the port bay, with two Chandler's hovercraft parked there.

I spent more time on the bridge those days, because it was one of the few places where there weren't several people looking at me oddly.

"Do you ever long for the good old days, Flax, when we

had time and privacy to talk about personal things?" I asked Flax.

"You mean like last week, Star?"

"Yes, Flax, like last week."

"It was different, but then I don't eat or sleep. The increased population affects me little. There is more weight taking off, but once up to cruising speed, I take no notice. No one has come into the console to bother me. Do you find the extra population to be an inconvenience?"

"Well, I'd like my room back, but considering that these people have lost everything, it sounds a little fussy to say so."

"All will be well once we set down on Shu. You'll see. It will all work out."

"Thank you, Flax, you are a comfort."

I had been aboard long enough to feel slight changes in speed or direction. Now I felt both.

"Why are we changing direction, Flax? And did I feel us speed up?"

"Yes, Captain. I did increase our speed and changed trajectory."

Flax was usually not so tight-lipped. Rarely did I have to ask what was happening. She would open up and tell me without hesitation. Now she was being close and cryptic.

"Well? Why did you change speed and trajectory?"

"Three reasons, Captain, and all of them are vessels. Wait."

Flax hadn't said that in a very long time, not since we lost all power in the middle of nowhere. Knowing that when she said wait, the best thing I could do was to wait, I sat there, my muscles tensed.

"Hi Star, what's the latest?" said a voice behind me. I jumped nearly out of my skin. It was Dione, climbing into the co-pilot's seat.

An odd feeling came over me, I had been here before, felt like this. It was new and yet it was comfy and familiar. Yes, because usually Chineel would climb into the co-pilot seat. Now Dione took over the position. She didn't know she was walking on hallowed ground.

"You surprised me!" I said, to explain my reaction.

"Sorry. Were you thinking?"

"Listening. Feeling. We just changed direction and speed. I asked Flax why and she asked me to wait."

"Wait?" asked Dione.

"Wait," said Flax in the same flat voice, the one she used when she couldn't use valuable CPU time being cordial.

"So we're waiting," I said to Dione.

She had come a long way, the young, chipper sergeant of the Icarus Constabulary. She was ready for anything and changed direction in a heartbeat if needed. When Captain Vikare put on his uniform to assail the Serapis Peacekeepers, he didn't even have to issue orders to her, he just strapped on his sidearm and turned to find her fully dressed and armed, ready to go.

"You know," I ventured to say, as long as we were waiting. "It's fine with me if you stay with us after Shu. We're going to a planet where no one has started a colony. It will be an adventure of grand proportions. I think you'd like it."

"This is all coming at me kind of fast. I don't even know what the options are to consider."

"Consider this, you don't find your place in the universe, you carve it out, sometimes with your bare fingernails. Bacchus just could be where you do that."

"I'll consider it," she said, putting all thinking on a side burner until later.

We looked out at the darkness, as the stars twinkling. I glanced at one of the rear screens. There was a dot on it that didn't look right.

"Is that it?" I asked. Dione turned her head, but I wasn't talking to her.

"That's one," replied Flax.

"How many more?"

"Two that I can see, big though."

"Markings?"

"None I can discern, no signal from them. One seems to be following us, which I just confirmed. It changed course and picked up speed to match our own. The second seems to be following him and the third, following the second. If we go off the edge of space, these three will probably go off after us."

"It's strange to be followed this far into the outer reaches."

"Yes, it is, Captain."

Flax raised her head over the console and the three of us watched the stars and contemplated the vessels following us through the emptiness of space, space that was getting crowded.

Battle Gear

Klack!

The familiar sound woke me. It was the wood on wood of the fighting sticks, the quarterstaffs Dagon and I used to keep sharp and pass the time between ports.

Klack! Klack!

"Oh!" cried out a dozen voices.

Klack!

I stumbled out to the starboard bay to find our passengers, young and old, sitting in a circle while Dione Ariadne and Dagon fought in the center. Their faces reflected both glee and sheer determinism as they danced around each other, sticks at the ready, seeking an advantage.

Klack! Dagon brought his stick around to Ariadne's head. Ariadne blocked, her stick at an angle from her left shoulder to a point above her right shoulder.

Klack! Ariadne countered with her stick to Dagon's midsection, blocked by his stick pointed down from his hands, perpendicular to the deck.

"Oh!" cried the crowd, me included.

I was in my dark blue silk pajamas, barefoot as I didn't have the time to find my slippers. Due to the overcrowding onboard my little ship, I had taken to sleeping in one of the bunks in crew berthing, whichever was vacant at the time.

Klack! Klack! Dagon sent twin blows to Ariadne, one side and then the other. Ariadne responded with a perpendicular stick, left and right, then...

Klack! ...a blow directly to Dagon's head, which would have split his skull, had he not blocked it with his stick upright and rigid in front of his face.

"Oh!" went up from the crowd in the bay.

An unseen communication crossed between the two fighters. They withdrew sticks, came to attention and bowed to each other.

The crowd applauded with a thunder to wake the dead. I turned and went back into the galley. In my universe, it was too early for stick-fighting.

Several other refugees stumbled from the sleep chamber to the galley to join me in morning ale.

"Good morning, Captain," said Aysu. She was dressed in a cut-down skirt once worn by Chineel with a blouse tucked in tight, so that it doubled upon itself at the waist. We were all making do these days.

"Oh? Is it morning?" I mumbled.

A child nudged a smaller child, sitting in the Captain's chair at the end of the galley table. The little one got up, embarrassed. He moved down the table and shared a seat with the larger child, still small enough to occupy half a seat. I managed a smile and sat down.

"It is if you say so, Captain." Hot morning ale appeared before me, steaming and aromatic.

"Quite a contest," I said. Around the table, gleeful faces smiled back at me.

A young man, younger than Dagon, at the far end of the table replied to me. "They've had no entertainment since we left our home in Juno. Once we set foot on Serapis, life became serious. There is no joy in Serapis."

"Well, this is Exterra Bacchus, where Flax is Master of the Helm and Starwort is your Captain. There is joy here."

All around the table faces lit up with smiles. These people had no hope and were getting some again. Seeing a test of strength and skill rather than forced brutalization of weak by strong brightened their hearts and lifted their spirits.

Dagon and Ariadne came in, still panting and sweating. Respectful children scurried to make room for them at the table.

"Well done, Dagon!" I said. "You've improved."

"Aye, Captain. Careful how you challenge me, you might find me a fit opponent."

"I will take care. And you, Dione. You know your way around a quarterstaff."

"Thank you, Captain. While most constables stuck to their blasters, several of us practiced on ancient weapons, tried and true battle-gear of the past."

"You both fought well. Aysu!" I called across the galley. "Hot morning ale for these two gladiators."

"Aye, Captain!" answered Aysu, bringing drinks for Dagon and Ariadne. Apparently everyone was going to start talking like pirates.

"What is the plan for the day, Captain?" asked Dagon.

"I will change, report to the bridge and see where we are."

Flax raised her head at the console. The children sitting around the table or on the floor against the wall all cried out, "Ooooo!"

"We are five days out from Shu, Captain. You must

make plans, which would include Captain Vikare, Dagon and Aristaeus. The rest of the compliment should eat and rest for the landing on Shu. The gravity is more than they will be used to. It is not noticeable, but after a time, one will tire faster."

"We'll pass the word," said Dagon, looking at Ariadne. She nodded, almost imperceptibly. It was the first time I realized that these two were growing closer, that communication was on a higher level between them.

It was like that between Chineel and me, and getting that way with Dagon and me. Words didn't have to be said; a glance would do the trick. A nod so subtle none other would notice. Abigail and I got to the point where we would look at each other simultaneously and know what the other was thinking. She would finish my sentences and I would finish hers. At times we would reply to a question or make mention of a situation with the same phrase, said at the same time.

Now Dagon and Ariadne were experiencing this higher level of communication. With a season or two at most between their ages, and both being experienced veterans so young in life, it seemed only natural that they would be drawn to one-another. Ariadne was a decorated sergeant of the Icarus Constabulary, trained with hand weapons and fearless in the face of danger. Dagon was the last survivor of a planet constantly at war. He was the first to jump into a fight and the one I counted on when danger was near.

In Juno, when we were losing a chase from men twice our size, Dagon stole a speeder and rounded us up, leaving our pursuers in the dust. It was that same speeder, the 'jumper' that he left on Khons, surrounded by troopers. If I didn't need rescuing, he would have fought them all for it. As it was, he stole a silver sphere and saved the day. The same sphere became Chineel's coffin. Every story connected to another story, some grand and glorious, some sorrowful and unhappy.

We were days from Shu and I still missed Chineel. But I was surrounded by friends and loved ones. I had filled Flax with a crew and now she brimmed over with people, twenty two souls.

Premonition

Once on the bridge, I settled into the pilot's seat. Captain Ares Vikare was already there in the co-pilot's seat. Doctor Aristaeus Genus was in the navigator's seat behind Vikare. I clicked the belt on the seat, as if preparing to take off or land, though we were nowhere near a port.

Flax raised her head above the console and smiled, looking around at the assembled faces. She looked up, anticipating another to join us. I turned to see Aysu wiping her hands on an apron as she folded herself onto the floor beside Aristaeus.

"Thank you all for coming," began Flax. I assumed that she had invited Aysu to join us. "We'll be at Shu soon. There are things we should know, some things we should pass on to others."

We all felt the importance of preparation for Shu, but also the presence of vessels in the blackness with us. We were not alone in our dark sky.

"We have met with two vessels in recent ports, a Free Vessel named the Kraken, captained by a pirate named Pytho. He has heard of treasure on a ship of which Starwort is the captain and is determined to garner it for himself. The second is the Ceberus, under Commander Belus, a particularly distasteful man, by his record. But he is determined as well. His mission is to capture the pirate vessel Kraken and another by the name of Bacchus, though the picture in the alerts does not match us. He is confused by the abilities of this small vessel."

Flax smiled. She enjoyed surprising those who underestimated her, and everyone underestimated her. She also knew that sooner or later, someone would realize that the genius of Doctor Genus was in her hardware and software, that the value of Flax's advanced knowledge and abilities far exceeded any treasure I still had. I was no longer the primary target of pirates and common thieves; Flax was.

"The third vessel is new to the game, the Minotaur,

Flagship of the fleet and home to Admiral Phanesh. His main interest seems to be the Ceberus, which he believes to be a rogue CG vessel. He seems to think that he will sweep up the Kraken and the Bacchus as part of the cleanup process, as if our vessels are part of the clutter left behind after an important battle."

A twinkle in Flax's eye told me she was having fun with these stupid men. Of the four vessels ours was the smallest and the only one without guns. If it came to a battle in space or on the ground using exterior guns, we would be completely unarmed. Our only defense was our exterior camouflage and diversionary tactics.

"Once we reach Shu, there are three possibilities for landing. The settlement is stretched across a wide expanse, but the landing platform is small and off to one side. If we land first, which seems likely at this time, we could be crushed by another vessel, as there would not be room for a second on the platform. We could then land on a wide patch of ground on the other end of the settlement, far from colonists and with room for at least those vessels we have seen up close. The Minotaur is a vessel that dwarfs us all. Where it will put down is a mystery, It might seek an orbit above and send landing craft."

I felt a shift in attention. Ares, next to me, felt it too. We both turned to see Aysu with her hand lifted, though not quite raised. Flax nodded to her. "Aysu," she said.

"In the wild zone, where the monsters are. That is where we will land."

"Yes, that is the third option, far beyond the settlement in the badlands, where the ground is rough and grows only brush and weeds. There animals we have not heard of are strange and unpredictable. In the wild place we will find great danger, but also great protection, because the other vessels and their crews will not venture there."

There was a space of time with only silence when no thoughts were spoken. I felt the pale, slender hand raise once more.

"We will face danger in the wild place, but the danger is less than faced by the crews of the other vessels." Aysu's eyes rolled back into her head and she went into a dreamlike state.

"The leader will fall. The smallest will rise. A mother hen will guard her nest, even on the far end of the universe."

Aysu fell over, caught by Dagon, who appeared behind her. He cradled her in his arms and looked at me. It was my signal to step in.

"Lord Khronos! We'll have to make sense of that, I suppose."

The mood lightened slightly as we all breathed again.

Flax took the lead, returning us to the tasks at hand.

"We'll need all the hovercraft, the RRD included. Though we do not know what will be outside the door, weapons are a good idea. We will need assigned crews. There will be a crew to go to civilization and make contact. Another crew will secure the vessel and a third will locate water. As you can imagine, our water tanks have been hard pressed to serve the many people aboard."

I stepped in to give names to those parties.

"Aristaeus will take Aysu to find water. Dagon and Ariadne will go with them for protection. Captain Vikare will safeguard the ship with the two constables and volunteers from the passengers as needed. I will go into the colony with Jessamine to make contact and find Papa Posey. He will be able to tell us the condition of the colony. We can then evaluate if establishing a foothold here is potentially viable or even possible."

"And what of the other vessels?" asked Aristaeus.

"They are the wild cards. We will have to see where they land and what their intentions are. You can be sure their intentions are not good."

"If the Central Government is here to take over, you can be sure there will be a rebellion."

"Than we'll be rebels as well as pirates. Any further questions?"

There were none. We went our ways, each with a new mission. I stayed behind.

"They are good people, Captain," said Flax.

"Yes, they are, and now they have something to do. Of all the detrimental activities in the universe, having nothing to do is the worst."

"What did you make of Aysu's trance?" asked Flax.

"She did that before. Leaders falling doesn't sound good, smallest rising is what happens when leaders fall. New leaders don't just get appointed when the universe is the battlefield; they rise to fill the empty boots."

"The part about the mother hen has me at a loss, but then I have little experience with them. They are more of a rural, domestic reference. Do you make any sense of it?"

"No, Flax. Unless it is an allusion to captains and their ships, or mothers aboard and their children. You can read into it, but I suggest we just keep watch until the situation arises and know she was speaking about that."

"You are wise, Captain," said Flax.

"Let's hope, so, Flax. Let's hope so."

Shu

As children on Khons, we heard of Shu, the wild planet on the far edge of the universe. It was not actually the far edge of the universe, it was just the far edge of the part we had the audacity to say we had civilized. In fact, nothing was civilized. Some places were under control and others were not; it was that simple. Shu was not.

Being far and desolate, the Central Government sought to establish a penal colony, a place to put the worst prisoners to relieve their overcrowded prisons and increase the punishment at the same time. Three giant freighters were retrofitted with extra air, water and fuel to go from Earth to Shu. Each was filled with prisoners.

None returned. The rumors were that the Central Government had found a new way to deal with political dissidents: put them in a ship and send it off into space, never to be heard from again. No one doubted that the CG was capable of such an act.

Improvements in vessels made the idea practical and eventually a ship of selected prisoners did arrive on Shu. They found a strange planet filled with hitherto unknown pitfalls and unpredictable perils.

Soon colonists seeking a life out from under the Central Government's thumb began venturing farther and farther from the central planets until they came to Shu. Little was known beyond that.

This was the world we were entering.

The landing place we had chosen was far from the nearest settlement out in the feral zone. Updrafts and strong air currents made the approach tricky. I sat helpless in the pilot's seat as Flax guided us in with experienced skill. Still, we were buffeted about like a child's balloon. Twice, Dagon had to retie the secure lines to the RRD. Anyone not strapped into a seat was in danger of flying across the bay.

Whether it was an overcast day or simply cloudy all the time, I couldn't tell, but it was difficult to see the terrain below us. Flax drew a three-dimensional map over the console of the place where we descended. It was craggy and rough, dry and windswept.

"Is there anyone to notify of our landing?" I asked Flax.

"I have been sending hails at regular intervals with no response."

"Then the answer would be 'no.' What is it like out there?"

"As I mentioned, breathable air is thinner, 88% of what you are used to. Gravity is slightly higher, but unnoticeable at first. You will tire easily until you become acclimated."

"Is there movement below us, Flax?"

"Do you mean flora and fauna?"

"Exactly. Is there any wildlife?"

"Yes, Captain. There is a great deal of wildlife, much of it moving away from the site where we are about to set down. To the local denizens, we have already been announced by our noise and air-disturbance."

"Well, we do make a fuss when landing."

"It is a space vessel, it is expected to make a fuss."

"What kind of a day is it, Flax?"

"Heavy coat weather, Captain. It's time to take out the gloves and scarf. A wise man would bring goggles and a breather."

"Then let's be wise. Shall I announce?"

"Yes, now is the time."

I reached to the main console, to one of the few buttons I knew, one of the few I was allowed to touch, though the captain, and selected the announcement setting.

"Now hear this, now hear this, all passengers and crew to your secure stations, we are about to land. No one is to open doors without instructions."

I gripped the arms of the pilot's seat as Flax lowered us down to the surface on thrusters.

As we dropped below the cloud cover, I saw a land of black and tan, dry and rocky, with spires sharp as knives and mounds of round rock as well. Mirrored reflections that then rippled as we dropped further showed me pools, hopefully of water.

"I see pools below, Flax. If the clouds are of water moisture, we might have the makings of a rain system and water pools."

"The clouds are indeed of water moisture, Captain. I tested them on the way down. The pools you see below are water, teeming with wildlife. I suggest further testing before you attempt to drink it, or even touch it."

"Good advice, Flax. Can you detect anything poised to jump us?"

"No immediate threats, Captain, though I sense a vehicle leaving the nearest settlement and heading this way."

"Let's hope it's a welcoming committee."

"Perhaps you should take side-arms, just in case."

I slipped out of the pilot's seat and through the crowded bay and galley to the crew quarters. There I changed into my battle-gear, my armored unitard with heavy boots and great coat. With gloves and woolly scarf, goggles and breather, I must have looked a sight.

As Flax settled in her chosen spot, I walked to the bay door. I was joined by Captain Vikare, Sergeant Ariadne and Dagon in full battle array. My ears told me Flax was testing things, soil, air, temperature, wind velocity and so on. She was making sure there were no unknown dangers for her captain, crew and passengers. When the sound stopped, the door opened.

Fresh, new air, even at 88%, was welcome in the cramped space that was home to twenty-two, originally meant for nine.

I stepped out onto a crunchy ground. My feet sank two inches beneath my weight.

In the distance, a dust cloud announced someone coming at a tremendous rate of speed. As the speeder drew closer, I could see that it was a closed speeder with a crystal dome. Inside was a black man, not unlike one I had once called friend. Next to him was a person I could not discern, as he was completely covered.

The speeder skidded to a stop not far from me and I

was waved over. I walked to the speeder and was addressed through the sound system as a voice came from small speakers around the dome's base.

"Are you Central Government?"

"No, we are a free vessel."

"Are you pirates, then?"

"No, we are mostly refugees from Victoriana and Serapis."

"You are mad to land here. Use your thrusters and follow me."

The speeder's driver swung his vehicle in a wide circle and stopped, waiting for Flax to follow.

I returned to the bay and on to the bridge as the bay closed behind me.

"Flax," I said, lowering myself into the pilot's seat.

"I heard, Captain. Engaging Gull Drive."

Quiet and slower, the Gull Drive made less fuss as the ship moved. We could follow the speeder without much trouble. I wondered who I was speaking to.

"He reminds me of Osiris from the Wind Pools, Flax."

"He doesn't give off the same wave," replied Flax.

Aysu came up to the bridge and stood in the space between the seats, her hand on my shoulder. She looked at the speeder ahead of us.

"He is suspicious, curious and wary, but he is not a danger."

"That's good to know," I replied.

"There is less noise here, less than the resort, less than Earth, even less than the ride out. I can hear things better."

Aysu stood as if listening, keeping a hand on my shoulder.

The speeder took us to the edge of a settlement of many single-story brick structures. A small crowd was assembled in front of one of them. The speeder came to a place which was flat and smooth. It circled once and then moved off to set down. Flax read the motion and set down on the flat place. When the door opened, there stood the occupants of the speeder.

Shu, named for the ancient Egyptian god of the air, followed in the tradition of naming things for the history, and at times, the mythology of Earth. That which was lost on Earth would be preserved in the planets and colonies it spawned.

But the people of Shu didn't care to follow the artificial tradition for long. Though our official greeter was named Emanuel, his daughter in the seat beside him, was named Aqua, for life-giving water.

"I am Emanuel, the leader of this village. This is my daughter, Aqua. We welcome you, if you come in peace." Emanuel eyed the blaster at my hip with some suspicion.

"We do come in peace. I am armed because I didn't

know what would be outside the door when it opened. Please forgive my ignorance."

"There is no need. Come, we should get inside, there will be inclement weather. We will tell you about the planet where you've landed and you will tell us of the world from which you came."

We left our weapons and armor behind, along with our misgivings about the people of Shu. Twenty-two people followed Emanuel into the largest building as Flax closed up and settled in for the coming weather. Few people noticed a twenty-third figure among us, dressed in a replica of my summer skirt and blouse. It was a little over thirty feet from the vessel to the meeting place and she had no difficulty projecting that far. Flax settled between Aysu and Jessamine. She fit right in.

Invasion

While we heard about the covered fields, the fenced food bins and the huddled brick houses of the settlement of Eastmost, due to its location relative to the rest of the settlement, other vessels were landing.

The Kraken lowered itself down on the main landing platform of Shu, boldly throwing open its bay doors to reveal a barren wasteland before him, completely lacking in people or life of any kind. Pytho, holding a blade in one hand and a blaster in the other, but with no one to intimidate, felt lost. He stepped out onto the flat, black platform and walked to the edge. The air seemed to glow around him and the ground seemed to pull him down.

High above him, the enticing song of a gorrache was heard. The most beautiful bird of Shu, the colorful plumage stood out in sharp contrast to the dull, brown landscape. The prominent bill was larger than the bird's head, which was made for crushing large shells and husks.

Agni stepped out of the bay door of the Kraken and looked up at the colorful bird flying toward him in a series of flits and starts. He raised a hand to catch the bird, offering it a perch to sit on. The gorrache perched instead on his shoulder. Agni smiled and looked at Pytho.

"Look, this bird's perching on my..."

The gorrache grabbed Agni's neck in a vice-like grip, opening the carotid artery. He drank deep of Agni's blood, as the doomed first mate fell to the ground. Agni writhed for a moment, unable to shake the bird, then died.

Pytho fired his blaster at Agni, killing the bird but reducing Agni's head and neck to cinders.

"Where have we landed?" asked Pytho, to no one, as he looked around at the landscape.

Two miles to the east as the gorrache flies, Central Government Fleet Vessel Ceberus settled down on a field of green surrounded by low buildings on three sides. The fourth side of the field was bordered by low hills covered in scrub brush. As the main door opened, the First Mate of the vessel stepped out, took a deep breath and turned back to the bay.

"It's breathable, sir. You can come out."

Captain Belus stepped triumphantly out of the door, his hands on his hips, ready to receive the surrender of the leader of this community, whoever he may be.

"There's no one here, Ensign Amun. Why is there no one here?" asked the Commander.

"I don't know, sir. There was supposed to be people living here."

Belus stepped off of the platform onto the green and sank up to the knee. He screamed and floundered, waving his arms madly. Amun and two other officers jumped in to support him.

"What is this, Amun?" screamed the Commander. "Some sort of crop, sir, they are growing food."

"Well, they shouldn't grow it in the middle of a landing area. Find someone, we need to talk to someone."

Amun dispatched four officers to the buildings on the fringe of the growing field.

"Crops!" muttered Commander Belus, making his way back to his ship, assisted by two crewmen. "The first thing I'm going to do is to burn this field. Get me out of here!"

Three miles further east, as the gorrache flies, the Minotaur, a vessel three times the size of the Cerebus settled down on a flat spot on the edge of a village. The two huts nearest the chosen landing area were destroyed by the thrusters as the vessel landed.

The main door opened and two airmen of low rank were pushed out onto the ground. They were carefully watched on the monitoring screens. They seemed to be standing and breathing well enough, they didn't turn a strange color, nor did they collapse upon entering the atmosphere.

"State your status," came orders from the craft.

"Stable and livable, we are in no distress."

"Return to the vessel." The door opened again and the crewmen were allowed into the airlock. After the door closed, the air was normalized in the airlock and the crewmen were allowed into the main part of the ship where they were examined by a medical team.

Meanwhile, Admiral Phanesh stood at his station looking out over the vast colony before him. As far as he could see across the valley, rooftops of single-story dwellings filled every space with only narrow walkways between them. He could see no roads, no vehicles, no maintenance buildings and no airship hangers. There were no space vessel bays. No Central Medical facility was in evidence, no visible headquarters for the Central Media or offices of the Central Government. The Admiral could see no sign of real civilization.

"These people are completely ungoverned, uninformed

and uncared for. How can they live?"

"Admiral, the Ceberus is three miles to the west of us. Not far from the Ceberus at the main platform is the unaffiliated vessel, Kraken."

"What of the vessel the Ceberus was following?" asked the Admiral.

"Disappeared completely, Admiral. Location unknown. Indeed, existence unknown. It may have been burned up upon entering the atmosphere."

"Keep scanning. I want to know everything. Assemble a party to go into those mud huts there and bring back a leader of this stone-age throwback."

"Immediately, sir!" snapped Technical Ensign Eanush, the Admiral's nephew and right-hand-man.

"And get me Bubak!"

The crewmen standing near Admiral Phanesh went pale.

"Uh, sir," stammered Eanush. "Shouldn't we learn more about the situation here before we disturb Bubak? He's in Cryo, after all. Once we terminate Cryo-sleep, well, he's awake."

The Admiral turned to his unnatural offspring and lowered his brows. He spoke low and slow, so that even the idiot son of his whore could understand.

"Bring - me - Bubak!"

The Admiral looked back at the field of low buildings

and exhaled loudly, as if expelling his past mistakes from his body. The crewmen closest heard him murmur, "I should have put the boy in the engine room, hauling trebium scuttles."

Below the houses of mud brick, in a labyrinth of tunnels under the main colony, the younger children were being shown to the lower levels by the older children while the men and women of Shu were arming themselves against the invaders.

Storm

In the large meeting house on the edge of Eastmost, we prepared for a storm. Flax moved closer into an indentation in the nearby hill, protected from the wind, and dropped her anchor foot. Bays and hatches were shut and sealed.

Emanuel supervised as the door was closed and the windows shuttered. Children were urged to the center of the great room and sat with their mothers.

The powered lights around the sides of the room were extinguished and candles housed in glass globes were lit. In minutes, the room took on a warm glow.

As if on cue, thunder sounded in the distance. The

sound of rain on the roof followed. Emanuel settled in between me and Vikare.

"The children are not afraid. They have heard a storm before."

"So, they're common?" I asked.

"Oh, yes, every few days. After a while we learned to make the streets run downhill so that the water will follow and go to the fields. We have planted rice of many varieties. It loves the water."

A flash of light outside found its way through the crevices in the shutters. A crack of thunder followed, making the children jump.

"Of course, they still jump at the thunder." Emanuel smiled.

The people in the meeting room were of every sort, every color. People of different Earth descents did not gather in groups, as I had seen in other settlements. Here, they mixed freely.

"So, Captain," began Emanuel. "Since we are here for as long as the rain falls, tell us a story."

"What kind of story?" I asked. It was a strange request.

"The story of why you are here."

"Oh, that." Perhaps it was not such a strange request after all. "I have heard of Shu since I was a child, that it was a wild land filled with wild things, animals I could not imagine. Then I heard a friend of mine say he was coming here to live where the Central Government could not reach. His name is Papa Posie. Do you know him?"

Emanuel looked at me for a long moment. I couldn't tell what he was thinking or what effect my words had on him. Then he looked to the center of the room, at the children gathered there. Thunder rolled outside as the rain beat against the settlement.

"Papa Posie is one of our wise men. He lives now in the main village. He is growing older and is looked after by those adept at healing."

"Is he ill? He is an old friend and I remember him fondly. His friend Jessamine is also with us. We would like to speak with him."

"So you do not mean him any harm?" asked Emanuel, looking directly at me for my reaction.

"No, not at all. Out meeting will be one of joy and remembrance. He will be happy to see us."

"Then we will go as soon as the storm is over."

A woman, pale and slender, bent down from behind us to whisper in Emanuel's ear,

"Other vessels have landed on Shu. How many are in your party?" Emanuel asked of me.

"You see them here. You saw our vessel. That is everyone in our party. What is known about the other vessels?"

Emanuel turned to his daughter. "Aqua, bring Kilian to me."

Aqua stood and stepped over several children to get to the other side of the great ring. She whispered to a handsome young man, who got up and followed her to us. He was soft brown with sandy hair and blue eyes. He wore shortened trousers and was without shirt or shoes. His bare chest rippled with muscles and his hands were strong and calloused.

"Kilian, tell us of the vessels," said Emanuel.

Kilian dropped to the floor with his legs crossed, as if he was settling in to tell a long story. Aqua sat by him and put her hand around his back.

"There are three, each larger than the last. One is a ship is twice the size of the one just landed, with the likeness of a hydra-head on the bow."

Emanuel leaned in to me. "He means a snake. We have no snakes on Shu so he has never seen one. We do have a many-headed monster with mouths filled with teeth. We call it hydra." Emanuel returned his gaze to the young man before him.

"The second is larger still and sits in our most productive rice field. The third is the largest and has landed outside the southern village. They have sent soldiers into the out-buildings."

"Thank you, Kilian." Emanuel turned to me. "So, they

are not with you. Do you know their purpose?"

What could I tell him? That we have brought oppression and destruction to his doorstep? That I am death and hell follows with me? I had come in peace, but three of the most evil-intended and heavily armed vessels in the universe came with me.

It was Flax who took up the conversation.

"We saw these vessels in our screens, but they were far from us. We did not know they would follow us all the way to Shu."

Seated between Jessamine and Aysu, Flax sat like a fine lady at an afternoon social. She looked at me and smiled, the innocence of a babe reflected in her countenance.

Aysu picked up the conversation, not as in a trance, but as if she was at tea with friendly neighbors.

"We have seen the little one before, though certainly larger than our tiny vessel. He seems to have an interest in our captain. I believe their captain is intent on learning if she has any fortune that he could make his own." Aysu leaned forward, as if it was a secret. "I think they're pirates."

"Very interesting, young lady," said Emanuel.

"Aysu. Pleased to meet you."

"And you as well. And the other vessels? What do you know of them?"

"They are official vessels, government ships, armed to the teeth and full of bad attitudes," said Flax. "They are not here for treasure or to be cordial. I think they have come because you are not run by a Colonial Governor. If they appoint one, it will not be from among your number."

"No miss, you're probably right." Emanuel looked around at Kilian and Aqua, then at several other adults in the circle. "It seems we have some challenges ahead of us, my friends."

"Please tell us what we can do to assist you," said Flax.

Emanuel turned to me. "Captain, does this young lady echo your thoughts as well?"

I stood to answer, taking a heroic stance, though with a summer skirt and blouse, it felt strange to do so.

"Yes, Emanuel, she does. If we brought this pirate vessel to your planet, we are embarrassed and apologize. As for the rest, we are at your service to help as we can."

"Who exactly is in your active crew, Captain?"

"We have a crew of eight, including myself. The rest are refugees from several places. Most are tradesmen and craftsmen. Some, as you see, are mothers and children. We have two with experience as constables. One is a soldier. And then there's me; I have been known to create an ache in the side of those who oppose me." I twinkled at the suggestion, taking delight in the idea that coming up against me would result in a painful experience. To see myself as dangerous and colorful always brought a smile to my face.

"We will endeavor to stay on your good side, Captain Bacchus."

"Please, Emanuel, call me Starwort. My friends call me Starwort."

"Then I will do so as well. But for now," Emanuel was interrupted by rolling thunder. It shook the building and made the children to huddle together, their eyes like saucers. It continued for longer than I was used to. When it faded away, Emanuel continued. "But for now, we must learn more about these visitors. Kilian, send your friends to learn of these strange, new vessels."

Bubak

On board the Minotaur, Bubak, the man named for a monster of Earth myths who sews garments of human flesh and rides in a cart pulled by black cats, was woken from a long sleep. This one didn't wear garments of flesh or ride in a cart pulled by cats, but was a giant with distorted features and uncontrollable temper. Placed in cryogenic sleep until he could be put to use, he was brought out now by Admiral Phanesh. His new mission was to instill fear in the local population of Shu.

"Admiral, this man killed three crewmen for merely looking at him."

"Don't look at him, Eanush."

"He was put in cryo for a reason, sir."

"Yes, Eanush, he was put in cryo for this reason. He will save lives. In fact, he will save your life. He'll go out and quiet the population of this village so you will not have to."

Technical Ensign Eanush shut his mouth, knowing his Admiral was right; the threat of Bubak would do what he and a dozen mere troopers could not do. The villagers would quail in fear of the ugly, angry giant.

As Bubak was brought out of his deep sleep, rations for seven men were put on plates and shoved down the table toward him using long sticks. He stood half a man taller than the tallest man aboard and twice as wide. His hands were the size of three and could crush a man's skull with ease. His face was scarred and irregular with remnants of ill-healed broken facial bones. His teeth were overly large and uneven. At the sight of him, children screamed and women fainted.

"He is a monster, sir!" whimpered Eanush to the Admiral.

"Yes, Eanush. He is my monster! See that he is armed and sent into the village to bring back the leader. Inform me when it is done."

The admiral turned on his heel and left the bridge.

He went to his stateroom at the rear of the vessel, looked out of the vast wall-high windows at the rugged landscape of Shu and rang the orderly bell.

A diminutive man in a short white coat arrived. "Bring me a pot of tea," said the Admiral, not even turning to acknowledge the man.

The orderly bowed out of the room, leaving the Admiral to contemplate what he would call his new planet, once he had brought it under submission.

"Phanesh. Yes, Phanesh would be a nice name for my new planet."

Suckers

After Kilian was dispatched to learn more, the conversation turned away from invasion and toward more immediate and pleasant topics.

"The rain is abating, Starwort. Will you show me your vessel?" asked Emanuel.

"It would be my pleasure, Emanuel. To do so, I will invite my friend, Flax, to join me."

I raised my hand to indicate who I meant and Emanuel's eyes fell on the stately figure of Flax. As he did, Flax stood, turned to him and walk through three people to stand before Emanuel, who smiled.

"So one of your party is a hologram, and a very lovely one, if I may say."

"Thank you, Emanuel. It is my pleasure to convey these people to your lovely planet. Please allow me to show you around the vessel I am."

The rain had lightened up and the day was brighter. Emanuel and several of his friends followed us out. Flax had released the Exterra from the protected indentation and it was sitting outside of the meeting hall on the edge of the landing space. The bay opened as we stepped out. Flax extended a graceful arm.

"Welcome to Exterra Bacchus, a free vessel, though not a pirate," said Flax.

"You have no armaments," said Emanuel. "I should have noticed that right away. I apologize."

"No need," I said.

A sharp scream caused us all to turn. One of the Serapis children had cried out. Fringed, reddish lifeforms had attached themselves to the young boy's bare arms and legs. The boy stood in terror, screaming in pain.

"Squirt!" called Emanuel. At once, a young lad from his village ran to the boy with a bottle. He pressed the sides of the bottle and liquid flew out in a spray. The strange lifeforms shriveled and fell away. One of the village mothers brought salve to cover the boy's bites and the boy stopped crying.

"Suckers," said Emanuel. "I suppose the rain brought them out. I apologize, we forgot you are new to the dangers of our lands. Shu children are immune to them. The bottle contains salt water, which they cannot stand.

Just don't get between the little ones and the parent. A mother hen will guard her nest, even on the far end of the universe."

"Yes, I've heard that," I said. I glanced back at Aysu, who blushed but didn't say anything.

"There are many strange lifeforms on Shu that will gladly feed on human parts, blood, fat, toenails."

"Toenails?"

"Apparently. You will see several adults missing toenails."

"Ugh!" I said without thinking.

"Yes, that's what we think as well. But we don't have insects that sting and give deadly diseases, We don't have poisonous snakes or giant birds that eat carrion, large cats that could kill a man or crocodiles in our rivers. We have heard that there were borths sent here to guard prisoners, that they escaped to the wild when the prison failed and are still out there, living in packs. We have not seen them."

"That's going to give new life to a thousand Wild Borth Attack stories told by escaping soldiers."

The boy, Kilian, ran up to Emanuel and spoke in his ear. Emanuel smiled and thanked the lad.

"Would you like to meet your pirates? We know where they have landed."

"I'll get my blaster," I replied.

Confrontation

The RRD bounced over the uneven road, the hovermags doing little to even out the bumpy ride. The rain had slacked just enough to allow us to pass. We sought to get the drop on the pirate vessel before they knew it had stopped raining.

Dagon sat next to me, armed to the teeth and holding his quarterstaff with both hands. Behind me, Captain Vikare and Sergeant Ariadne, holding her quarterstaff as well, did their best to stay on during the jarring trip.

Behind the RRD rode the Chandler's vehicle, filled with volunteers. We were going to meet the pirate who ruled the vessel named The Kraken.

The Kraken of old is part history, part mythology, said

to be a squid or cephalopod of tremendous size. It could wrestle a whale or bring down a sailing ship. It is believed in later years that such an animal would only attack a ship believing it to be a whale. Whether a kraken actually existed or not, the description and stories told in the galley frightened everyone. The concept that these pirates were after my vessel and crew frightened me.

We slowed as we drew near the landing platform, stopping behind a wrinkle in the ground tall enough to hide the vehicles. I waved the volunteers to stay low and stay hidden while I took Dagon, Ares and Dione with me. We were about to walk into the Kraken's lair.

As we walked across the barren ground to the landing platform, I saw the bay door open. Figures were inside looking out, though still standing in the shadows. While we sized them up, they were also sizing us up.

At the edge of the landing platform, a gun port opened and the cannon inside trained on us. I made a motion with my left hand. Ares and Dione moved to my left.

Another gun port opened; another cannon found a target. I made a motion with my right hand and Dagon moved further to my right.

A third gun port opened, targeting Dagon. We each had our own pirate gun trained on us. I felt special.

Within earshot of the bay door, I stopped. Dagon, Dione and Ares stopped at the same time, as if we had rehearsed it. Behind me, I felt the eyes of a dozen volunteers as they looked over the rise in the landscape at the pirate ship. From a viewing port high on the vessel, a glint of light told me someone was watching and was aware of the dozen defenders ready to join the fray should it come to that.

"I would speak to your captain," I called out to the bay. No response came.

I looked around behind me at the dozen in reserve and moved my head ever so slightly. The hovercraft came around the rise raising a cloud of dust. It pulled to a stop behind me. A dozen armed people got out and extended the line the four of us had made. Sixteen determined faces told the pirate ship we weren't kidding.

"Your captain!" I repeated.

Fifteen ragged crewmen, some in remnants of uniforms from the Dark Side of the Moon, stepped out of the bay of the Kraken. They stood in an uneven line in front of the vessel, looking unsure about whether to attack, defend or run away.

Down the ramp, dividing the group and making a show of it, came the man I assumed to be the captain. He was taller than the rest and two gun belts at his waist and one across his chest. He had on a Central Government officer's short coat, no doubt taken during a past adventure.

"I am Captain Pytho," he said. He assumed a heroic stance that would have brought derisive laughter had we not been faced off and heavily armed.

"I am Bacchus, captain of the Exterra you have been tracking across the darkness. Why have you been seeking me?"

"Your ship is of value, as are you, Captain. You hold an inheritance of great treasure, I hear. So I would have it for mine. Come aboard and negotiate with me, there may be a chance for you to save your people and make a home here, for yourself and your crew."

"You misread the situation. Do you believe that we are in your custody?"

"We are sixteen even, but add to that three cannon. We can blow you from the sky deck, and would without hesitation."

I took a breath, just a quick one, in order to deliver whatever I had prepared to say next, but never got the chance. Another stole my thunder.

"You cannot give that order, for you are no longer Captain of the Kraken."

The Challenge

It was Ares who threw down the challenge, stepping two paces forward as he did.

"If not me, who? I was not informed of a regime change. Who has deposed me?" roared Pytho. He looked around, expecting chuckles of derision from his men, but they were silent.

"Captain Ares Vikare, of the Icarus Constabulary, and I challenge you for the right to command these men and this vessel."

Everything stopped, even the air hung in the sky. If there were birds, they had ceased their flight. No breeze disturbed the dust, no passing animal scurried for fear of upsetting the delicate silence. I had forgotten to breathe.

A laugh broke the stillness. It was the pirate leader.

"I accept your challenge, Captain."

Captain Pytho stepped forward, removing his bandolier containing a large blaster as he did. He took another step forward, taking off both gun belts. Captain Vikare also stepped forward, removing his pistol and holster, laying them on the sky deck.

The fifteen pirates stepped back, giving their captain room to fight. I motioned my people back as well. Captain Vikare had made his decision and we had to respect it.

Captain Pytho took a long knife from his belt and dropped it on the ground. Captain Vikare removed the blade from the left side of his belt and dropped it as well. Another step and the pirate Pytho grinned, held out both of his hands and stopped. He was showing that he had shed himself of all weapons.

Captain Vikare also stopped, held out his hands and glared at the pirate. In that instant, I had a thought: Vikare was never all that bright.

As fast as a snake striking its prey, Captain Pytho reached to his boot, brought out a three-quarter sized blaster and fired point blank at Vikare. Vikare flew back, a hole in his chest. He fell onto the sky deck and didn't move. Pytho grinned. A single grunt escaped his lips, a grunt like a laugh.

A high scream went up from my left as Sergeant Dione charged the pirate captain, her fighting stick raised high. She covered the distance before the pirate could comprehend that a real danger came toward him. He looked up, raised his pistol at the advancing Sergeant and crumpled as Dione's stick came down on his head.

Dione recovered and delivered a blow to his side, to the other side and then to his back as he bowed to the ground. One more blow to the skull made the blood shoot from the open gash in a spray onto the sky deck.

Dione stood over the dead pirate captain, her fighting stick ready. For another moment, hearts stopped and all was still.

In the distance, I heard the call of some animal, a tick-tick-tick of another and a slight movement of the breeze, barely disturbing the air.

"Well done, Captain!" said the nearest pirate.

"Your orders, Captain?" asked another.

"We are yours to command, Captain," said a third.

Dione looked at the line of pirates. All were bowed before her, their hands to their weapons, but not as a threat, rather in tribute. Dione Ariadne had bested the pirate chief and was now the Captain of the Kraken.

Sword Play

The Ceberus sat in the rice field as the rain subsided. The men sent into the village to find the local leader did not return.

"Commander?" said the port lookout. "I think you had better come and see this."

Commander Belus, rolled his eyes and twisted his mouth. What could it possibly be this time? He walked to the port lookout station and leaned over the rail into the observation bubble, looking where the crewman was pointing. At the edge of the green field, made higher by the recent rains, four posts had been erected. Each post held one of his men, tied. Next to each, a figure stood holding a sword.

"Swords?" said Commander Belus. No one had used swords in battle in centuries. Any swords in existence were in a museum, behind glass, under lock and key.

"Should we fire, sir?" asked a crewman.

"No, don't fire. No firing. Let's find out what they want."

The commander didn't care about the crewmen, they were expendable. The Central Government recruited extra crewmen for such vessels, knowing that a certain percentage would be lost in first encounters. The Ceberus left port with a fifteen percent loss already noted in the log; only the names of the fallen were missing, they were yet to be added. No commander cared about the first fifteen percent. It was curiosity that drove him, he wanted to find out what the rebels wanted.

At the first post, Dagon held a sword half as tall as he stood. He had no doubt that he could wield it quick enough to decapitate the man at the post and three more advancing on him. I had no doubt either.

At the second stood Captain Ariadne of the Kraken. In her hand was a sword taken from the extensive weapons locker of the Kraken. The Ceberus crewman at the post whimpered a pitiful wail. He knew the determination of the captain who held his life in her hands. So did I.

I stood at the third in my battle gear, the armored unitard that kept me protected, warm and allowed me to maneuver at the same time.

Having never wielded a sword, I was unsure that this would be convincing enough. I did have my larger blade strapped to my thigh, not under skirts as I often carried it, but outside, for all the world to see. If the sword wasn't convincing enough, that blade in my practiced hand should send shivers up the most hardened trooper's spine.

Emanuel stood at the fourth post. This was his land these people had invaded and he was not to be left behind. Emanuel, strong, tall and jet black, with large eyes and pearl-white teeth, was a fearsome figure to behold.

Under orders from its new captain, the Kraken settled in on the low hills behind the rice field, its guns trained on the Ceberus.

No gun ports opened from the Ceberus, no cannons were trained upon us. I took it as a sign that the pirate vessel had been seen and that wisdom won out over bravado.

"Can I help you?" came a hail from an exterior loudspeaker.

"Step out, captain, we cannot see you," yelled Emanuel. His low, rumbling register commanded more respect than Ariadne's soprano melody or my alto harmony. Dagon was too angry to speak, much less yell. It would have come out as a battle cry and the man at the post would be the first to hear it, though it would be the last thing he would hear.

The senior officer was taking his time. Several scenarios to deal with the delay went through my head. Flax could tell I was considering action.

"Wait," she said in my earpiece.

The bay door opened. From inside a small man stepped, frightened as if facing danger for the first time. He wore a Captain's coat and insignia, but was lost in them.

"Um, I'm the captain. What do you want?" he quailed.

"You are an idiot and will die an idiot's death very soon. Send out your real commanding officer, spindleshanks, e'er I slit your throat second." Emanuel's words made me smile. He had a way.

The diminutive crewman Emanuel had called 'spindleshanks' spent no time returning to the depth of the vessel. In time, a pompous senior officer too long absent from the gymnasium stepped out of the bay and down to the edge of the vessels loading plate.

"I am Commander Belus. Who demands my attention?"

"Two captains, a governor and a soldier worthy of

respect. Step off, Commander. Wade the bog and meet us at talking distance."

"You're insane! I'm not getting in that!"

"You decision," said Emanuel, holding the sword up to the throat of the crewman tied to his post. The crewman made a sound like a squawk.

"Wait!" cried out the Commander. "Wait, wait, just wait. Just... wait!" He made a difficult decision. His crewmen or his trousers.

It was a tough one. I could tell he made a lot of difficult decisions in his position. I shook my head in disbelief. My small, silent statement was not lost on the Commander. He stopped, one foot in the bog and one still on the loading plate, and looked directly at me. I could almost hear him. Who was this girl, this child, to smirk at him?

Silently, I answered him: Hesitate once more, Commander, and I will show you the resolve of this girl, this child.

The Commander stepped off and waded with difficulty through the bog up to the post where Emanuel stood.

"I'm here. Release my man."

"Only if you take his place, Commander."

"You're mad! A nameless crewman for a Commander? You think me a fool?"

"Yes!" I said, making the Commander turn his head to

me, the child who had smirked. "But that has nothing to do with our discussion. Come over here and receive your orders."

The Commander looked at Emanuel. He had waded in green muck quite enough for one day and wanted to rain destruction on these people and be done with it.

Emanuel raised his eyebrows and tilted his head. The simple, subtle movement said, "Well, get moving."

It was the longest three steps of the Commander's life, but at last he stood before me, awaiting my edict.

"You will pack up your crew, secure your guns and leave this planet," I began.

"I will not!" protested the Commander.

"I'm not done!" I said, more like a petulant child than a ship's captain. "You will leave this place and never again think of the vessels you have tracked here. You will return to Earth's skirts and there hide until you retire, old and beaten. This is now our sector and you have no part in it."

"You have not heard the end of this," said the Commander.

"And you have not asked about your crewmen. Do you not care about them in the end?"

A long pause said mouthfuls to the four standing crewmen and those still within the ship. It seemed a millennium before the Commander spoke again. When he did, it was without interest.

"Yes, of course, what about my crewmen?"

"If they choose to, they may return with you, unharmed. But if they choose to remain on Shu, they will disappear into the population and you will never find them again."

"Keep them! I don't care. Slit their throats and see if it changes things. It will not."

The Commander turned and walked toward his ship. It was slow going across the bog. As he trudged, up to his hips in green muck, I cut the bonds on the crewman I held.

"Your choice. Follow your commander or remain here, but make it now."

"Yes, Captain. On your orders," said the crewman with a snap salute.

The other three were released but no one made a move toward the ship. High on the Ceberus, air vents closed. The loading platform and bay door also closed, leaving the Commander knee-deep in bog and not yet aboard. The ship was securing for takeoff.

I drew back. With me, three comrades and four new refugees pulled back also. The thrusters started and covered the cries of the Commander. As they spewed fire into the rice field, the Commander fell and was consumed in the blast of the liftoff.

The Ceberus rose in the air and launched high up to the sky. The last we saw of it was a dot in the sky as it found its trajectory to Earth and set a course.

Predictions Confirmed

As we returned to the village, to the large meeting room, I leaned in to speak to Emanuel.

"I would like to find Papa Posie"

"He is in the center village. He is a revered storyteller. You may not get an appointment to see him."

"I'll get an appointment. We go back a long way."

The man named for the god of the sea was indeed on Shu and was waiting for us. He had told the story many times of his valiant escape from Khons and the young friend he left behind, the closest thing he had to a daughter. The soldiers came to the house when he was gone and took Jessamine captive. He returned to find the empty house. An escape vessel was leaving for Shu and he left with it. We would go soon to reunite father and daughter, but first, celebrations were in order.

In the main meeting room, food decorated seven tables and drink was being poured. Together, we had rebuffed the invaders, the pirates and the troopers alike. Future generations would gather around storytellers and hear of the exploits of this day. The names of the fallen would be spoken in hushed tones.

In truth, there was only one fallen comrade: Captain Ares Vikare, the man who called out a pirate and died through foul play. Aysu's prediction had been correct, the largest had fallen and the smallest had risen to take the lead. Captain Ariadne of the Kraken had done her part.

My eyes fell on Dagon, no longer with a child's down softening his cheek. He had fulfilled Aysu's words as well, he was becoming a man before our very eyes.

I thought of the final words of her prophecy, "The man will find a home and the orphan will have a family." Whether the man was Aristaeus, Runyon or any of the other refugees Flax brought to Shu, they would find a home, here or on Bacchus. As for the orphan, it could mean me. Is this the family I was meant to have? Aysu could have easily meant Jessamine, or herself for that matter. We were all orphans.

I leaned over to Aysu and touched her hand.

"You were right, Aysu. Your predictions are coming true."

Aysu smiled but her eyes said she was unsure if this was good news or bad.

As we prepared to raise our glasses, news of a new vessel reached us, a Central Government ship larger than the last, an admiral's vessel, a behemoth, the flagship of the fleet.

Thinner air and increased gravity made me tired before I was ready. I left the party and was shown to a room far from the revelers, where the sounds of the celebration would not wake me. There I dropped into the arms of welcome sleep and was warmed and comforted with rest and renewal.

Full Battle Dress

The lack of sound woke me. The party had at last come to a close, the lights were extinguished and the last of the revelers had retired to their rooms. once again, I dropped off to sleep knowing all was right with the world, at least the one I was in.

The creak of a door stirred me. A shaft of light passed across my closed eyes. I opened my eyes and allowed them to become accustomed to the darkness. A figure was standing against the far wall. A quiet shuffle, as if far away, told me he was finding his place, adjusting his feet and preparing for his announcement.

The man against the wall opened the creaking door

with his left hand, pulling it fully open. The light from the hallway flooded the room. I saw him in the light. He was a CG officer holding a blaster. A knowing smile was on his lips and his eyes were lowered to half-lids. Getting the drop on me was more than he had hoped for.

"I'm Commander Moloch of the Minotaur, Captain Bacchus, under command of Admiral Phanesh, and you are under arrest. Sit up, Captain."

Sleep still held me in its grip. My mouth was dry and my head unclear. I sat up enough to see the man against the wall more clearly.

"I have you at pistol-point, Captain. I suggest you surrender without a struggle."

"Drop your gun!" said a voice behind the Commander.

The Commander turned in an instant, but met only the wall, scraping his hand. His blaster fell to the floor and clattered across the room to my feet. His face smacked the wall, breaking his nose. A loud "crack" echoed off the walls. He crumpled, holding his face with a bloody hand, searching for his pistol with the other.

"I have it here, Commander. You are my prisoner now," I said.

The Commander looked at me wide-eyed as the change of situation sunk in. He looked around at the wall for the source of the voice. As he did, she stepped out. It was Flax, in full battle dress. She stood half in and half out of the wall facing the disbelieving Commander.

"Manacles, Captain," she said to me.

I stepped over to the huddled man, took the manacles from his belt and pulled his arms behind him, attaching the metal bonds tightly.

"Give me a minute," I said to Flax. I was dressed only in a nightgown, my feet were bare.

"There is no time, Captain. Follow me."

Flax passed through the Commander, crumpled on the floor, and walked to the door. The Commander fainted as the person who just turned the tables on him walked through his body. He had not prepared himself for an enemy who walks through walls.

I followed the holographic Flax down the hall to another sleep chamber. She motioned me to wait, pressed against the wall.

Emanuel walked out, his hands bound. With him were two armed guards and a senior officer.

Flax stood firm in the center of the hall, her holographic blaster aimed at the officer.

"Hold where you stand!" said Flax.

"Drop your weapon," I said to the officer, who turned with a surprised look.

Seeing a girl in nightclothes holding a CG blaster was not in his experience. He hesitated for a moment, but the look of wicked delight on my face caused him to decide on a safer route. He laid the weapon on the ground and raised his hands.

"There's a manacled commander in my room," I told Emanuel.

"You have impressive troops, Captain," he said, with a glance to Flax.

Emanuel crept down the hall to the main room, where the party was held the night before.

"Where are there more soldiers?" I whispered.

"I expect they are being held..."

"As you are," said a loud voice from behind me. Three troopers with blasters had turned a corner to find us unready. Flax stepped between us and faded away.

The pistol was taken from my hand and from Emanuel. We were lead out to the main hall where several others of our band stood against the wall at gunpoint.

As the troopers pushed me against the wall with the others, I saw that I was not the only one with bare feet and dressed for slumber; several ladies were in nightgowns, two men were in underclothes and one was draped in a blanket. Seven more had fallen asleep in their clothing and were now rumpled and embarrassed.

"Help is on the way," said a voice in my head.

"I know," I replied, also in my head. It was Abigail's voice. She had found me and had managed to slip into my consciousness. I did know help was on the way, in many ways. Abigail was with me, though she would say she is with me always, and Flax was lurking close by, ready to surprise someone by walking through the walls.

"Clever girl!" I thought.

"Flax is clever," said Abigail. "She has a body that is not, yet is. Clever girl!"

Eight soldiers joined us. The Commander came from the hallway straightening his uniform. His face was bright red as he took his pistol from the Captain, patiently holding it out to him.

"Show them out, Captain," ordered the Commander.

The Minotaur's Captain smiled at the Commander's embarrassment, but he turned and raised a hand, indicating the door to the outside.

The rough sand and small stones were sharp to my feet, but I used the pain to further wake me up to my plight. These soldiers had us at gunpoint, but I had weapons they didn't know about. One was my childhood friend, Abigail. Another was Flax who had vanished along the way to the hall. And there were others not yet taken captive. I expected them to jump out and create another turn of events, but there was only silence outside.

The Bubak

Outside of the great hall, the early morning breezes made me shiver in the thin nightgown I had donned for sleep. We stood as if waiting for something as yet unnamed and unknown. I expected to see the vessel I had heard about, the largest of them all, appear and land in the square. There wasn't room in the square, but it was something I could think of.

The Commander stepped up to Emanuel.

"You are the leader. Tell me: Where are your people?"

"You see them here before you. Less than a dozen and one is a visiting captain." replied Emanuel.

The Commander glanced at me and smirked. I was

short, barefoot, dressed in a flimsy nightgown and topped by a tangled mass of hair. I did not impress him as a heroic figure.

"They are few, but they are mighty," said Emanuel. The Commander didn't answer. Instead he raised a hand, summoning someone as yet unseen. The ground shook as the steps of feet the size of speeders drew near.

"Behold Bubak, feared by all men!" said the Commander, as if the giant coming toward us was a wonder of the universe.

"Stop!" whispered Abigail.

I heard her, but I wasn't doing anything.

"Stop, Bubak." The giant stepped into the square, but then stopped, looking around him.

I realized she wasn't talking to me, she was talking to Bubak. I was just listening in.

Flax stepped out of the wall of the main hall. Three soldiers turned their pistols on her. Flax flew into a crouch, one hand poised over the blaster envisioned at her hip.

The three troopers fired at Flax. The blasts went through her to the wall behind, riddling it with holes.

Yet Flax remained untouched. She stood up, laughing, yet without sound.

The sound came from behind and it was not a sound, but a scream.

Dagon came flying from behind the main hall, his fighting stick in the air. He struck the first trooper, dropping him to the ground. The second turned his blaster on Dagon, but was dropped by a swipe from his fighting stick. The third crumpled under the full weight of the stick on his head.

The Commander looked about him with confusion. From the other direction, Runyon, Jessamine and Aysu charged from the side buildings. All three held blasters and fired them at the feet of the remaining troopers, who fell to the ground holding their wounded feet.

Flax walked to Bubak. With every step, she grew, until she stood eye to eye with the giant.

"You have no fight here. Your fight is on that vessel, with the man who held you captive."

Bubak took in the words, narrowed his eyes and turned around. He strode through the village causing the ground to shake with each step.

Two-dozen troopers crossed the plain in formation and double-time. They saw Bubak walking toward them and stopped. An order was given by the Sergeant in charge and the troopers returned to the vessel, triple-time.

Bubak entered the vessel and screams came from within.

Standing next to me, the Commander regained his composure and reached for his pistol. His eyes targeted me as the source of all his troubles. He would soon be rid of this impudent child.

"You have lost your fight, Commander," said Abigail in the Commander's head.

The Commander's resolve failed him and he turned pale, dropping his weapon and putting both hands on his head. He fell to his knees and banged his head with his fists, trying to force the unwanted voice from between his ears. Emanuel stood over the broken Commander and gave one last edict.

"Order your remaining men to carry the injured to your ship, Commander."

The injured men were lifted and carried out of the village to the waiting vessel. Inside the vessel, the deep, frightening roar of Bubak mixed with high-pitched screams as he exacted revenge against the Admiral of the Fleet.

"Captain?" said Emanuel, offering me the Commander. I stepped up to the Commander and pulled his tunic, bringing his face down to my level. I looked him in the eye.

"I'll tell you what I told the other commander, the one of the Ceberus: This is our corner of the universe. You have no place in it. If you return..."

"It will upset me and I will turn you insane," added Abigail from within the man's head. None of the troopers heard her, they only saw the man's eyes grow wide with fear as the blood drained from his face. He had been walked through by one ghost, talked to by another, his giant had been turned and his behemoth of a ship had been bested by a rag-tag team lead by a diminutive girl in a nightshirt. It was enough for him.

"Keep it, then, Captain. You have spirits and banshees on your side. I want none of it."

The Commander turned to his men and barked his orders.

"Into the ship, prepare for takeoff." He turned to regard me one last time. "Set sail for Central Headquarters. We must report this quadrant closed to future traffic."

The Commander turned once more to his crew, still barking orders: "And secure Bubak! Get him back in Cryo!-sleep!"

Reunions and Goodbyes

On one side of the grand table in the main hall of Shu, I sat with Aysu and Dagon, no longer a boy-soldier. He was now a man, as Aysu predicted.

Across from us, Aristaeus, Papa Posey and Jessamine sat. Emanuel held forth from the head of the table. Runyon and the rest of the Serapis refugees took up a section, while Captain Dione Ariadne of the Kraken occupied another. With her sat the constables who came with us from Serapis and several of the pirates, who it turned out were previously staff at the lunar resort.

"We have to discuss the keys to Bacchus, Papa," I said to Papa Posie.

"But you already have the key, you have come from your home in Khons. There you found that Jessamine, with whom you shared the Jasmine Tea Ceremony, was at the lunar resort. There you found her and also Aysu, the seer, the teller of truths. You have brought a boy across the universe and now he is a man. You have been followed by and have bested a pirate ship, a ship-of-the-line and an Admiral's fleet-ship. And you have a friend who can not only convey you through the space inbetween, but can step off the vessel and throw the switch to open the route to the green side of Bacchus."

"Flax?" I said, not sure what he was saying.

"Oh, Galium! In his secretive way, he probably couldn't tell himself that the key to Bacchus is that you must pull the lever without getting out of your vessel, as it is in the vacuum of space that the switch lies. It is on the single circling moon."

Papa Posie smiled, leaned in to Jessamine and imparted a secret. "The moon around Bacchus has no name, it is only known as 'the Moon,' much like another we know."

"It's a switch?" I said in disbelief. "On the moon?"

"Oh, it's a switch or a lever or some such. It has been told to me in so many ways. The difficulty lies in that you can only land at the platform and cannot move from there unless this device, whatever it is, is enacted. But you must activate it from the moon that circles Bacchus and to do that you must be outside your ship. But how can you be outside your ship and not die? You see the conundrum?"

"Yes, I do. It is up to Flax to step out of the ship and activate whatever it is that is on that moon. She couldn't do that before Aristaeus gave her a full form to ramble in. Thank you, Aristaeus."

"You are both welcome."

I stood up to deliver a speech not yet written or thought of.

"Friends, we have come a long way across the universe. From Cecrops to Khons, the place of my birth. Then to the moon of Earth, to Serapis and here. There have been challenges and some losses along the way."

A catch in my throat made me pause as I remembered that Chineel had been lost along the way. But she would have wanted us to go on and so we would.

"We have a long way yet to go, some of us. A new challenge awaits us on the planet Bacchus." I looked at Dione, small but tested and proven, and wondered if she would come with us. I hoped she would.

"My friend, Galium," a low murmur went through the room. "Yes, the most wanted man in the universe, but still, my friend, told me of a green part to Bacchus and it is large, fruitful and a paradise. Now I know the key, so I plan to go there and make it my home. I am taking a few with me."

Dagon and Aysu beamed up at me. They would come, but others would not.

"Shu is a good place, with good people. Any who want to stay, will have my best wishes for your success. Those who would like to meet the challenges of Planet Bacchus, are also welcome. We have limited space on Exterra Bacchus," a giggle rippled through the assembled crowd. "As you know. But we'll find a way. To those who remain behind, we thank you for your help and for your love and will always hold you in the highest regard."

I sat down to applause from all around the table. I expected Emanuel to stand next, but it was Aristaeus who took the floor.

"Starwort, my dear friend, I send Flax with you and charge her to watch over you always. I'll miss you, but my place is here."

With Aristaeus's tender words, I thought I saw Flax grow misty and thought she was going to tear up. But Dione took the floor with unexpected words.

"Captain, if you don't mind. I have told the crew of the Kraken my mind and have consulted with them concerning their desires. If it is agreeable with you, our intent is to rename the vessel the Icarus and to sail to Bacchus with you, to build a peaceful colony there."

I rose and went to Dione, who met me halfway. We shook like captains, then hugged like sisters. When we drew apart, we both had tears in our eyes. The entire table rose with applause.

Emanuel said wonderful words, I'm sure, but I was overcome with emotion and some sadness. I had gained loved ones, but had lost some as well.

At the end of the celebration, Emanuel came up to me.

"You didn't hear a word I said."

"I know your heart, Emanuel. We have no need of words."

"Very true, Starwort. Is that really your name?"

"Yes, it's the name of a flower. The starwort flower is medicinal, it heals pains in the side."

"Or sometimes gives it, I think."

"It has the significance of afterthought and grows in shallow waters." I pulled at the collar of my blouse revealing the flower tattooed on my shoulder-blade.

"You carry it with you?" said Emanuel.

"It's to remind me not to stay in still waters, lest they grow stagnant."

"If you ever find yourself in stagnant water, you will find free running springs on Shu. You will always have a place here."

"Thank you, Emanuel. If you find yourself seeking new scenery, consider Bacchus. We hope to have it up and running soon."

"I can think of nothing that will be able to stop you."

Emanuel put his arms around me and held me for a long time. It was good.

New Orders

"New orders, Sector Agent," said recently promoted Sergeant Shem.

From the corner, behind a stack of ancient boxes filled with cold-case files from the archives, the beaten eyes of Constable Phaeton looked out with apathetic dullness.

Sector Agent Honor Toth took the reader and pressed a thumb against the pulsing red dot at the bottom of the screen. In an instant his new orders came up.

"From the Central Government Headquarters on Earth, direct orders from the Supreme Leader, Seb. As the Sector Agent, Honor Toth, has proven more effective than other agents or methods in tracking the fugitive, Galium, he is directed to the coordinates believed to be his destination. A shuttle capable of such a range is to be issued to him immediately, along with a crew of his choosing, to find, apprehend and bring in this enemy of the state."

It was signed by the Master General of the Central Government Constabulary Forces.

"Sergeant Shem, can you fly a shuttle?" asked Honor.

"Yes, sir, I can," grinned the sergeant.

"Then find me a vessel that will take us to these coordinates and assemble a team to fly the vessel. Make sure you take your favorite people, Shem, as we may be gone quite some time."

"Aye, Sir," snapped Shem.

The Sector Agent looked at the coordinates, then up at the big screen, where the map of the sector was displayed. There in the corner was the planet that sat at those coordinates.

"Bacchus," said Honor Toth with a smile.

~ *End* ~

About the author...

Jon Batson is an award-winning author, four-time winner of the Lower Cape Fear Short Story Contest, twice awarded Honorable Mention in the internationally known Writers of The Future Contest for science fiction writers and twice in the Rusty Axe Science Fiction Contest. He makes his home in Raleigh, NC.

For more information about Jon Batson and to purchase his other books please visit:
http://www.TheRealJonBatson.com
jonbatson@live.com
midnightwhistler@gmail.com

Also by Jon Batson

Adventures of a Space Bum 1
Starlost Child

When Starwort Bacchus finds herself running from her landlord, skipping out on the rent, she jumps aboard an automatic repair vessel and hitches a ride to the next port. But the search for her father's legacy, the inheritance her uncle nearly decimated, takes her to planets where friends and enemies are hard to identify, and her best ally is a computer. With a pocket full of "Universals" and a ceramic blade strapped to her thigh, she travels the darkness looking for a home. Instead she finds a growing list of places she cannot go to again, including a place she has never been – Earth.

Adventures of a Space Bum 2
In Search of a Legacy

Starwort continues her search for her father's legacy, carefully avoiding an ever increasing Central Government presence, an epidemic virus spreading from planet to planet and the constant threat of those who seek to steal the legacy. To her and her crew, the promised haven of a home planet seems a dream they will never realize.

Adventures of a Space Bum 3
Finding Galium

Starwort searches for her early ally Galium on a planet with a resort city, home to a criminal mastermind, an energetic constabulary and an active wedding location, where she meets an old friend. When they come together with Starwort and her crew, the fireworks are spectacular.

Mars Quake

When astronomer Dana Wright thinks she has seen writing on Mars, she wants to take a look through a larger telescope. Senate aide Tom Matthews knows more than he is telling. Tom remembers every one of his past lives and all the people who shared them with him. That is, until he meets Doctor Wright, someone he's never met before. His memory, whether Doctor Wright likes it or not, is the key to the new markings on the Martian surface.

Blue Standoff

When police detective Max Cole buys a DVD from the $2 bin at the discount store, he has no idea that the plot of the movie would parallel his current case, right down to the ex-girlfriend.

The Trasaron Chronicles
Fade to Black

When Earth's population is relocated to a work planet, three unlikely heroes emerge to organize a resistance, dedicated in retaking their home – Earth. This character driven sci-fi saga takes the reader on a page-turning adventure exploring survival, interpersonal relationships, and quality of life.

Deadly Research

When author Jack Richmond researches his next novel, he uncovers the biggest conspiracy in history, happening under our noses and in plain sight. Now Jack and his girlfriend are running for their lives. Deadly Research is the first novel in the Jack Richmond series.

Research Triangle

Jack Richmond discovers a building on the edge of the Research Triangle where school children are being remotel monitored from a distance for medication reactions. The monitoring room was joyous at the killing of 32 students until the discovery that they were being recorded. Jack wakes with no memory at all.

Terminal Research

The story continues as Jack Richmond returns home on Halloween to find that his fiance, Teri, has been abducted. Finding her becomes his first objective, but along the way he has to deal with new assassins, old friends gone bad and members of the organization really running things.

Doll Bodies

Out-of-this-world tales including other possible futures, space stories, and excerpts from two future full-length projects. If you are craving a little Sci-Fi in your day, here you are. Enjoy!

Nina Knows the Night

Nina Richardson, a mild-mannered law school dropout, is tired of the criminals in her neighborhood. She dresses in black and ventures into the night to become a kick-butt crime-fighter. She discovers her superpowers to be her own inner-strength and purpose.

What they're saying about Jon Batson:

"Jon Batson is not just a writer, but a storyteller. His gift is making you experience what his characters feel and see while he slings irony and witty asides that make others wonder why you're laughing so hard. He looks closer at the ordinary world and determines what extraordinary things a person can do given the right circumstances. The result is a story that won't be put down."
Alice Osborn, author, editor and teacher of "Write from the Inside Out."

"Colorful, engrossing, and highly entertaining! Jon Batson has produced an evocative collection of engaging characters whose lives unfold in amusing, tragic and, often, unexpected ways that send the imagination gliding over each one's winding paths, hairpin curves and jarring potholes with the artistic finesse of a truly masterful storyteller."
Karen Michelle Raines, poet/author

"Batson's stories are contemporary yet reminiscent of an earlier time. O'Henry, Raymond Carver and Edgar Allen Poe come to mind. Luckily for us although the aforementioned have gone onto their last edit, Jon will be with us for a long time."
Steven David Elliot, Entrepreneur

"I could hear you in every sentence. Easy reading, nice payoff, and a few surprises."
Gary Young, Author

Made in the USA
Charleston, SC
28 October 2016